Betrayed!

They broke from the strangling vegetation of the jungle and raced across a field of waist-high grass. Hardly turning his head, McCarter took a barely perceptible look at Manning, who was nearly abreast of him. Manning nodded just as unobtrusively, and they both continued to probe their surroundings with flat and concealed sweeps of their eyes.

Ahead of them by about fifty yards, their guide kept throwing quick looks over his shoulder, then peered to his left, where the rain forest lay dense and seemingly deserted.

Suddenly McCarter's eyes caught a fragmentary flash of pale sunlight glancing off some reflecting surface deep within the foliage, and in the same moment the guide turned abruptly, lunging for cover.

Seconds later the forest ahead echoed the blast of full-auto fire as the Phoenix mission suddenly went hard.

Mack Bolan's

PHOENIX FORCE®

PHOENIX FORCE®

GAR WILSON

AMAZON STRIKE

A GOLD EAGLE BOOK FROM

WORLDWIDE®

TORONTO • NEW YORK • LONDON • PARIS
AMSTERDAM • STOCKHOLM • HAMBURG
ATHENS • MILAN • TOKYO • SYDNEY

First edition May 1989

ISBN 0-373-61341-5

Special thanks and acknowledgment to
Michael Linaker for his contribution to this work.

1

The silence of the Amazon rain forest was shattered by a short burst of autofire that sent a stream of 7.62 mm slugs zipping through the dense foliage. Shredded leaves blew in every direction, and chunks of bark, chewed from tree trunks, pattered to the ground. The initial burst was the signal for other weapons to open fire, and for long moments the jungle reverberated with the harsh rattle of gunshots.

If the owner of the AK-47 that had started the cycle of fire had waited a few more seconds, the outcome might have been different. As it was, the intended targets simply melted into the rich undergrowth, leaving the ambushers to stare at empty space.

The mistake, however, had been made. The targets had to be relocated and dealt with. Recriminations could—and would—come later. A harsh voice rasped out a command, and armed men clad in camouflage combat uniforms burst from their places of concealment and began to advance in the direction of the vanished targets, weapons up and ready.

A single shot rang out from somewhere deep in the lush greenery. The 7.62 mm bullet lashed from the barrel of an FN-FAL assault rifle and struck one of the ambushers just above the right eye. It cored on through the man's skull and blasted off the back of his head. A sticky mist of blood sprayed the face of the man behind, who instantly dropped to his knees. Before he could even begin to wipe off the gore, a 3-round burst from an M-16 punched 5.56 mm slugs through his chest, splintering bone and ripping into his heart. Coughing up gouts of blood, the fatally hit man slumped to the ground.

The ambushers hesitated until the voice of their commander whiplashed them forward again. They broke into a run, firing as they moved, sending a deadly stream of gunfire into the foliage.

"ANOTHER FINE MESS you've got me into," David McCarter muttered darkly as he backed away from the advancing ambushers. Hot slugs sizzled through the undergrowth, some coming uncomfortably close to the British hell-raiser. He swung up his MAC-10 and sent a scything burst of autofire in the direction of the advancing enemy. He was rewarded by the sound of someone yelling in pain, followed by the crash of a falling body.

"You say something?" asked Gary Manning, the Canadian Phoenix commando. He stood a few feet to the side of the cockney hardman, his FAL sending deadly messages in the direction of the ambushers.

"I said I told you so," McCarter grumbled. "I was right all the time about that shifty-eyed bloke who was supposed to be guiding us through this bloody jungle. I said he wasn't to be trusted.'' The former SAS man gave a sharp grunt as a bullet seared the back of his left hand. ''Hey! That bloody hurt. You know something—I think these buggers are playing for real.'' McCarter plucked a grenade from his webbing and popped the pin, then he lobbed the grenade in the direction of the enemy. ''Heads down, chums!''

As Phoenix Force hit the ground the grenade exploded with a hefty crack. A dense cloud of shredded foliage and rotted vegetation from the jungle floor mushroomed into the steamy air, intermingled with a shower of human debris—the tattered remains of one of the ambushers who had been caught by the full blast of the grenade. The explosion temporarily halted the attackers' advance. They scattered, all military pretensions abandoned in the rush for cover.

With danger temporarily neutralized, the echo of the explosion still ringing in their ears, the five-man commando team known as Phoenix Force fell back to give themselves some combat stretch. Even as they penetrated deeper into the tangled mass of greenery, their minds were digesting and assimilating a single fact. They had been deliberately drawn into this ambush. They had been betrayed!

Yakov Katzenelenbogen, the unit commander, mentally reviewed their position as he pushed through the dense foliage, Uzi cradled against his chest. They had been abandoned by the man who they had been given to believe could lead them to their objective—

deserted in unknown, hostile territory and attacked by some paramilitary force that appeared to want them dead. It was not the most auspicious start to a mission.

Katz didn't allow the thought to worry him, however. Phoenix Force thrived on adversity; it seemed to bring out their best. To a man, they functioned best when the odds were stacked against them and the wall was at their backs. Already they had taken out three or four of the enemy force, despite being attacked without warning. Not that the game was over yet. In fact, it had barely started.

Phoenix Force's prime objective now would be to somehow elude the attacking force and then try to carry on with the mission—easier said than done, Katz admitted to himself as he heard the crackle of automatic fire. Bullets whipped through the foliage above his head, thudded into tree trunks. A lesser team might have folded in the face of such an attack, might have come apart at the seams, perhaps preferring submission to possible death.

But to Phoenix Force both options were abhorrent. They would only contemplate surrender when every other avenue had been exhausted. Death was the easy escape. Irreversible, it eliminated all other options. There was no chance for a rerun. So, being who they were, Phoenix Force chose the path that was as natural to them as breathing.

They hit back.

"Hey," Calvin James called out, "I thought the idea of this mission was for *us* to find *them*."

"Somebody changed the game plan," Rafael Encizo said.

"Well, I wish they'd call time-out," Gary Manning remarked.

"Uh-oh," McCarter said. "Here they come!"

The staccato rattle of autofire cut through the Brit's warning. Bullets snapped through the foliage, whacking timber. The moist air hung heavy with drifting powder smoke and cartridge casings glinted in the pale sunlight that filtered through the canopy of intertwined branches high above the forest floor.

With dogged persistence the attackers pushed forward, flanking Phoenix Force on both sides. Their numbers increased as more men emerged from the shadowed jungle.

Katz cut loose with his Uzi, the SMG sending a hail of bullets at the ambushers. The Israeli had lost an arm during the Six-Day War, but he had never lost his deadly accuracy. Two members of the unknown force were knocked off their feet as 9 mm slugs burned into them like hot pokers. They squirmed around on the forest floor, where the blood pumped from their fatal wounds was soaked up in seconds.

Around Katz the other members of Phoenix Force also returned the attackers' fire with controlled ferocity, asking and giving no quarter. Yet despite the Force's deadly response, the attackers began to overwhelm them, driving them farther and farther from the path they had been on, and deeper into the all-encompassing jungle.

"I don't think we're going to be able to shoot our way out of this," Katz yelled above the chatter of gunfire. He ejected an empty mag from his Uzi and jammed another home.

"What else can we do?" James asked.

"Don't ask," McCarter told him.

The former SAS warrior raked the green wall of foliage with his Ingram, blasting away vegetation and the human life it concealed. A man began to scream—a high-pitched sound that became increasingly shrill and babbling as agony overwhelmed him.

The attack force responded with a withering blast that filled the air with such a high concentration of howling projectiles that Phoenix Force was denied the opportunity to return fire. "Fall back!" Katz ordered. "If we stay here we're dead."

Foliage rained down on the Phoenix commandos as they pushed their way deeper into the undergrowth, each of them fully aware of his vulnerability in the present situation. The men of Phoenix Force were the best there were when it came to surviving, though each of them had suffered battle wounds from time to time during his career as a warrior. Each knew that every new mission he participated in might be his last. A bullet, or a knife, or the blast from a grenade could end the life of any of them at any moment. A man who refused to acknowledge his human frailty was a fool to himself and a menace to the men who fought alongside him. The Phoenix team always took time, if the situation permitted, to consider the effect on the rest of the team of any action being contemplated. If it put others at risk it would be abandoned.

As Katz considered the options, he came to the conclusion that the only action possible would be one that put them *all* at risk. Something had to be done before the remorseless rain of death pouring from the attackers' guns claimed the entire team.

"Stun grenades," Katz said. "They'll lose some of their effect in this dense vegetation, but they should at least make these guys slow down and give us a chance to get clear."

On Katz's command, five concussion grenades were activated and thrown. The resulting blast and bright flash and cloud of smoke screened Phoenix Force as they crashed through the thick curtain of lush greenery that lay before them like some living barrier. They ignored the slashing of thin branches, the sting of thorny hooks. Sweat burned in their eyes and plastered their clothing to their flesh. The breath began to catch in their throats. It seemed the wall of entangled foliage would never thin out. But it did. Suddenly.

They burst into the open, to be confronted by a forest pool, with a film of scum at its edge, roughly thirty feet long and thirty feet wide. The shadows of overhanging branches moved on the rippling surface. Insects hovered over the water, snapped at occasionally by aquatic creatures that splashed on the surface, then streaked to the hidden depths.

"Oh, shit!" Calvin James explained.

"And I didn't pack my swimming gear," McCarter muttered.

"It's flying gear we need," Gary Manning suggested.

The attackers had stayed right behind Phoenix Force. One of them threw a grenade, which struck the surface of the pool a microsecond before it exploded. Although none of the projected fragments struck a Phoenix warrior, the blast was enough to jar them. Encizo lost his balance, falling against McCarter. The pair plunged into the pool.

A volley of shots drove angry bullets in the direction of the other three. Gary Manning turned to offer a hand to the men in the pool, but as the gunfire threatened to end his life McCarter waved him off.

"Go on, get the hell out of here," the Britisher ordered. "Rafael and I can manage. You're no good to any of us if you get shot."

As another grenade exploded nearby, showering Manning with falling vegetation, he turned reluctantly and followed Katz and James, who were already shouldering their way through the tangle of undergrowth edging the pool. Seconds later he looked back and was unable to pick out the spot where McCarter and Encizo had gone into the pool. A cold hand clutched at his insides as he scanned the area. Nothing. His teammates had disappeared from sight. He hoped they had managed to conceal themselves. He refused to think about the alternative.

Up ahead Katz and James came to a halt. As Manning reached them he saw why.

A semicircle of armed men in combat gear faced the Phoenix warriors. There was no mistaking the grim expressions in their cold eyes. Katz and James had lowered their weapons. Manning did the same. There was no way the three of them could survive a close-quarter firefight with their trigger-happy pursuers.

"Put the weapons on the ground," ordered a tall man. He had broad shoulders and a lean, supple body. Beneath his combat cap his hair was blond, and the cold eyes that studied the men of Phoenix Force were hard and blue. "Now raise your hands, while we search for additional weapons."

"And then what will happen to us?" asked Katz. His calm manner and steady voice showed he was not intimidated.

The blond man smiled, but his expression was devoid of humor. "Then, my friend, you will become my prisoner."

Katz glanced at James, then at Manning, who gave a barely noticeable shrug. They all recalled McCarter's earlier comment.

Another fine mess you've got me into.

Another Stony Man mission. One more excursion into the hellgrounds, this time all the way to Brazil. A stark contrast to the subdued atmosphere of the War Room at Stony Man Farm. When Hal Brognola had started to outline the mission, they hadn't quite imagined the current turn of events. . . .

2

"We have a little problem," Hal Brognola said to the group assembled in the War Room.

The Fed was dressed in a rumpled suit and shirt. His collar was open, his tie loose, and he looked tired. He *was* tired. Weary but tense. He needed sleep the way a scuba diver needs air, but he knew from the way things were shaping that he'd get no rest for a while yet.

In the past twenty-four hours he'd set up a mission for Able Team and had then talked to the President for a long time. After that a dozen other matters had had to be taken care of, and now the briefing for Phoenix Force.

Yakov Katzenelenbogen sat on Brognola's right. The Israeli's appearance and relaxed manner did little to advertise the fact that he was one of the world's most accomplished antiterrorist fighters. He possessed a wealth of combat and tactical knowledge, gained firsthand from initially fighting the Nazi threat, then in Israel's difficult struggle for independence, right up to the present-day war against terrorism.

Across from Katz sat Gary Manning, sipping from a mug of steaming coffee while he waited impatiently for the briefing to get under way. Manning would have been happier back in the underground firing range, where he had been test-firing the new Enfield SA80, the British army's recently adopted service rifle. Firing the NATO 5.56 mm round, the SA80 was proving to be a tough, easy-to-maintain weapon capable of delivering its shots with deadly accuracy. Part of that was due to the weapon's optical sight, known as SUSAT—for Sight Unit, Small Arms, Trilux. SUSAT gave 4x magnification, and at night was illuminated by the radioactive Trilux light, again giving an advantage.

The SA80's bull-pup design, with the 30-round magazine placed behind the trigger, allowed for a shorter weapon length without detracting from its excellent performance. Over a period of time, Manning had put the SA80 through an exhaustive series of trials. And while he wanted to carry out even more experiments on the weapon, he had the feeling that the next tests he had planned were going to have to wait a while.

Calvin James sat next to Manning, with Rafael Encizo on his right. James, a tall black man, was the force's youngest member. The skill and daring of the ex-SEAL, plus his devotion to the ideals of Phoenix Force, had made James an invaluable member of the group.

The same was true of Encizo. A fugitive from Cuba, Encizo still dreamed of the day when the Communists would be thrown out and he would return to his island home. In the meantime the Cuban fighting machine used his knowledge and combat skill to aid the Stony Man campaign against terrorism.

Slouched in his seat at the far end of the table, drinking from an ice-cold can of Coca-Cola, David McCarter drummed the fingers of his free hand on the tabletop. McCarter hated inactivity. He craved action as other men craved wealth; action was what made life worth living for the former SAS man. Never one to take casual risks, McCarter did have a reputation for jumping first and thinking later. He was a natural, fearless fighter whose boundless energy and get-up-and-go attitude inspired others. When McCarter hit the go button it was a signal for everyone to move.

Tired as he was, Brognola noticed McCarter's ill-concealed impatience and quickly came to the point. He tapped the thick file lying on the table in front of him. "I've got tickets here for a nice little South American vacation."

McCarter flicked a finger against the side of his can of Coke. "I'll bet 'vacation' is just a nice way of saying we're going to be dropped into the jungle from a great height."

Brognola, unwrapping a fresh cigar, looked hurt. "Would I do that to you guys?"

"Is Spenser for hire?" Calvin James murmured softly, raising a general round of laughter.

"If I got you hotshots soft missions you'd complain even more," Brognola retorted. He glanced the length of the table in McCarter's direction. "Right?"

The Briton grinned. "Sure. Only joking, guv," he said, exaggerating his East End accent.

"We've got a line on a group based somewhere in the Amazon rain forest—" Brognola began.

"That's jungle to you," Gary Manning said to McCarter, who scowled back at him.

The Fed continued. "This bunch has been running a well-organized cocaine business that channels its product into the U.S. market. We have information from a Brazilian source that shows this group takes its payments partly in cash and partly in goods—goods as in weapons and military hardware, it turns out."

"Are they revolutionaries?" Encizo asked.

"Not exactly. They're a neo-Nazi organization."

Gary Manning groaned. "Not the *Mein Kampf* brigade all over again!"

"Those jackbooted idiots never stop crawling out of the undergrowth down there," McCarter said. "What do *these* silly buggers call themselves?"

"The New Order."

A smile creased Katz's face. "They can't even come up with an original name. Do we know who runs this group?"

"Yes," Brognola answered. "His name is Kurt Mohn—in his mid-forties. Been a Nazi all his life. His father was an SS major, a hard-line Nazi from the word go, who brought Mohn up in the belief that *Mein Fuhrer*'s way was the only way. It appears the indoctrination worked. Mohn has been active in the Nazi movement all his adult life. He's been in prison a few times, but he has powerful allies—wealthy Germans who are closet Nazis. Mohn disappeared from view for a year or so, then surfaced in South America again. Although he appears to be involved in operating his father's extensive legitimate business interests, which he, of course, inherited, the truth seems to be he's handling the affairs of this cocaine ring.''

"It's the weapons and hardware that interest me," Katz said.

"Yeah, what's the guy up to?" James asked.

"We thought at first the arms were for his own protection," Brognola said. "But there's been too much stuff going in."

"Maybe he's got an up-and-coming war with other coke producers," Manning suggested.

"Possible but unlikely," the man from Justice said. "Mohn has the field to himself in his area. There are no other gangs large enough or operating close enough to damage his operation."

"So what's our brief, Hal?" Katz asked. "Just to cut off Mohn's operation? Or do we dig deeper?"

"Both," Brognola said. "He's been shipping his drugs to the U.S. only, and we want that stopped, without question."

"And?" McCarter asked.

"Yes, let's have the bottom line," James said.

"Our contact in Brazil is Louis Farrango. He's a lieutenant in the police force, working a special drug squad. It was Farrango who initially connected Mohn to the cocaine operation. He's been working with one of our DEA agents to build up a strong enough case to bust Mohn.

"But Farrango ran into a wall. His investigations were blocked from high up in the Brazilian government. No names but plenty of interference—red tape. The word came down via Farrango's own superiors that he was to drop the Mohn case. This was just when Farrango had received information from one of his undercover men in Mohn's organization that there was something strange going on, something hotter than the drug business, that would eventually have worldwide repercussions.

"Farrango didn't know who he could trust. He'd told his DEA contact, of course, so the information found its way to Washington. In the meantime Farrango did the only thing he felt was left open to him. He went to the Brazilian president himself, in secret, and told his story. It turned out that the president had some suspicions about an organized clique, somewhere in his higher echelon, that was consorting with an outside group.

"It was around this time that the White House contacted the Brazilian president. The two head men discussed the matter and agreed that the only way to handle it was to put in a small group capable of putting an end to the Mohn deal on its own initiative. That way the Brazilian president wouldn't have to risk broadcasting his intentions to unfriendly ears. It's an awkward arrangement, but there doesn't seem to be any other way around it."

"We'll handle it," Katz assured the Fed.

"It has to be this way because there's no telling who, in the Brazilian government, might be in with Mohn," Brognola said.

"No problem." McCarter grinned wolfishly. "We just don't trust *anybody*."

Calvin James glanced at the British hell-raiser. "You make everything sound so damned easy. It's all just black-and-white, as far as you're concerned."

There was a momentary silence, then McCarter said, "Coming from you, that's bloody funny."

The two Phoenix warriors stared at each other, then burst out laughing.

When the laughter had faded Brognola said, "In a way David is right. We don't know who to trust. So viewing everyone as a potential enemy may be the only way." He pulled an 8x10 black-and-white photograph from his file and passed it across the table for Phoenix Force to study. "Don't trust anybody—except this man."

The photograph showed a dark-complexioned man in his early thirties, with thick black hair. A neat mustache adorned his strong-boned, intelligent face.

"This is Louis Farrango, your Brazilian contact. He'll be arranging the details of the mission and will brief you when you arrive in Manaus. From there he'll have one of his local informers guide you up-country."

"Not too happy about that," McCarter muttered.

"Nor me," Encizo said.

"We have to trust Farrango's word," Brognola said.

"His word may be okay," Manning said, "but how good is his man?"

Brognola sighed. "I can't give you any guarantees, guys. If I could you'd have them gift-wrapped."

"We'll just have to be extra careful," Katz stated. "It won't be the first time we've had to watch our backs."

"How do we get into the country?" Encizo inquired.

"By regular airline," Brognola said. "All your paperwork has been dealt with—passports for your cover identities, and so on. Flights are already booked. You'll arrive in two groups, posing as American tourists. Hotels have been booked, as well. Once you're settled Farrango will make contact."

"Weapons?" McCarter asked.

"They'll be shipped to Brazil as part of the diplomatic luggage from the Brazilian embassy here in Washington. Once they arrive the president will have them delivered to a safehouse where Farrango will pick them up and have them ready for you."

"All sounds reasonable to me," Katz remarked.

"Yeah?" McCarter said. "Then why am I getting that cold feeling in my stomach?"

Grinning, James pointed to the can in the Brit's hand. "Too much iced Coke."

"Ha-ha-ha." McCarter muttered.

Calvin James spoke up. "Assuming we carry this mission through, how do we get out fast if we need to? There aren't too many cabs in the middle of the Brazilian jungle."

It was Brognola's turn to smile. "Got a nice surprise for you." He picked up one of the telephones on the table and punched in a number. "Barbara? Yes. You can send him in now."

"Do we have to put on masks and try to guess who it is with twenty questions?" McCarter asked dryly.

Katz, lighting a cigarette, frowned at McCarter's sarcasm. The ex-SAS commando was often less than tactful when it came to stating his opinions or expressing his feelings. There were times when Katz could have cheerfully strangled the vociferous Briton. But then all Katz had to do was recall McCarter in action, storming through some red-hot firefight, with a gleam in his eye and a grin on his face. The sometimes abrasive Cockney was worth a five-man squad. He had a natural instinct for combat. At times it bordered on recklessness, and McCarter was frequently told off by others for allowing his impatience to get the better of him. He took wild chances, seeming to thrive on a razor's edge. He was the kind of soldier any man would want at his side during a battle: eager, totally fearless, a born fighter.

At that moment the door opened and Jack Grimaldi entered the War Room. A superb pilot, Grimaldi went way back in Mack Bolan's crusade against crime. After service in Vietnam Grimaldi had gone solo, flying for whoever offered the best rate. Without realizing who his employers were, he had become a wing-man for the Mafia. Then Bolan, already waging his one-man war against the savages, had come into Grimaldi's life. When Bolan lifted the veil from Grimaldi's eyes, enabling him to see with 20/20 vision into the cesspit of the mob, the flyer had cursed his own naïveté at being taken in by the syndicate con men. His disgust—directed as much at himself as at his evil employers—had quickly turned to rage, and a need to make amends. It had taken Bolan's unique insight into the human condition to wipe away the man's sense of guilt and remorse. From that day Grimaldi had served as a soldier in Bolan's War Everlasting.

During the long miles of those blitzing campaigns against the Mafia, Grimaldi had stayed with the mob, passing vital information to the Executioner. With the creation of the Phoenix project, Grimaldi had been one of the first to join. He had dealt himself in on Bolan's first Stony Man mission, pulled the Man from Blood out of a jungle firefight with a hurricane hot on their tail. Grimaldi had been on call ever since, using his superb flying skills to great effect on numerous occasions. McCarter raised his can of Coke as Grimaldi pulled back a chair and sat down. "How goes it, mate?" the Briton asked. An excellent pilot himself, David McCarter would have been the first to acknowledge Grimaldi's superiority.

"Never better, David," Grimaldi answered.

Greetings were exchanged around the table. "You're going to airlift us out of Brazil?" Katz asked.

Grimaldi nodded.

"I'd better take my motion sickness pills now," McCarter muttered, "to give 'em time to work."

Brognola ignored the remark, turning to Grimaldi. "Jack, give the guys a treat and tell them about Dragon Slayer."

"Who?" Calvin James asked.

Grimaldi opened the cover of the file he had brought with him and extracted a photograph. He handed it to James, saying, "This is Dragon Slayer."

"Man, I believe it!" James was looking at a color shot of a sixty-foot combat helicopter painted in a semigloss black finish. The unmarked aircraft stood about fourteen feet high, and its smooth, streamlined shape, with drooping nose and arched tail unit, did give it the configuration of the mythical dragon.

James slid the photograph across the table to McCarter. The Briton's eyes gleamed with unconcealed admiration for the machine.

"How fast can she go?" he asked.

"Had 320 out of her on a clean run," Grimaldi said. "With a full payload she'll still top 260."

"Weapons systems?" Manning asked.

"Rotary cannon in the lower nose with an optional laser-light sighting device. Rocket pods under each stub wing that can carry a mixture of loads, including heat-seeking missiles. There are electro-optical sensors on each wingtip to aid target location. Plus an air-data probe that sits up front. That measures airspeed, drift, angle of approach, and feeds the info to the onboard computer so it can calculate the correct firing coordinates."

"Impressive," Katz said.

"That's only the tip of the iceberg," Grimaldi said with a grin. "This baby's got so much hardware packed into her I haven't found it all yet. The Special Projects Department here at Stony Man who designed her didn't miss a trick."

"I've got only one question," Encizo said.

"Yeah?"

"Will it stay in the air once it gets up there?"

"Listen, Rafael," Grimaldi said, "that baby will fly with its ass pointing the way it's going."

"Oh, great," Encizo said. "If you don't mind, my friend, I prefer to fly the right way around."

They spent a little more time discussing the helicopter, but finally Brognola brought them back to the topic of the mission.

"Jack will be waiting for you at a fixed rendezvous," he told Phoenix Force, "ready to come in and get you if the need arises. Dragon Slayer's presence in Brazil will be explained as a sales demonstration by an American company hoping to sell the machine to the military. As far as anyone is concerned, Dragon Slayer is a design prototype. Jack and the helicopter will be flown to Brazil in an Air Force Hercules transport. He leaves tonight so he can have a couple of days in Brazil to put on a few demonstration flights, then he moves across country so he's near Manaus, which is where you guys are going."

"If everything goes according to whatever plan you work out, I'll come in and pick you up when you give me the word," Grimaldi explained. "In the event of any trouble I can still come in and pick you up, even if you've gone off track. All you do is activate one of these babies." He placed several signal devices on the table, each the size and shape of a pack of cigarettes. "They throw a signal Dragon Slayer can pick up as much as sixty miles away. Once she picks up the signal I start making sweeps until she homes in."

"When do we leave?" Katz asked.

"Three days," Brognola said. "So you have plenty of time to get organized."

"I'll have time to run those tests on the SA80, after all," Manning said with enthusiasm.

As they filed from the War Room McCarter drained his can of Coke.

"Make the most of that," Manning told him. "You won't get much of it in the Amazon jungle."

"That's what's worrying me about this mission," McCarter remarked solemnly. "No bloody Coke!"

Manning smiled. "Well, certainly not the kind you mean, pal."

3

Mr. Rubin and Mr. Blantyre stepped from the terminal building of the airport that served the city of Manaus and surveyed the line of taxis waiting there. Almost at once a white Mercedes sedan with a sign attached to its roof broke from among the parked vehicles and swept to a halt in front of them. The driver climbed out and opened the trunk of the car. He took the bags from the hands of the two men, placed them in the trunk and slammed the lid shut. Ignoring the protests of the other taxi drivers, who were casting doubt on his parentage, the driver opened the rear door of the Mercedes and ushered his passengers inside, then got behind the wheel. He gunned the motor and roared away from the airport, turning onto the road that would bring them to the city of Manaus.

The moment he had the car on a steady course the driver peeled off the dark glasses he was wearing. "Mr. Rubin. Mr. Blantyre," he said over his shoulder. "*Seja bemvindo,* Welcome to Brazil."

"*Muito obrigado,*" replied the man known as Mr. Rubin. "It's good to meet you, Lieutenant Farrango."

Mr. Rubin was in fact Yakov Katzenelenbogen; his companion, using the cover name of Blantyre, was Gary Manning. They were posing as tourists on vacation from New York and were booked into the centrally located Amazonas Hotel on the Praca Adalberto Valle.

Later that afternoon David McCarter would fly in from Brasília. Calvin James and Rafael Encizo were due to touch down about an hour later, on a flight arriving from Belém. McCarter, posing as an English playboy, was booked in at the most expensive hotel in the area, the Tropical. Overlooking the Rio Negro, it was about a forty-minute drive from the city. James and Encizo, in their roles as photographer and writer for an American travel magazine, had been given rooms at the Novotel on Mandii Avenue, which was in the commercial part of the city.

The splitting up of Phoenix Force was purely a precautionary move. It would divert attention from their arrival in the city. While there was no positive identification of the possible opposition, it was necessary to play a careful game.

And for this reason Louis Farrango was playing taxi driver.

"Your 'luggage' has arrived intact and is stored at my safehouse."

"Good," Katz said. "Has anything significant happened since we left the States?"

Farrango shook his head. "No. I am hoping to speak with my man on the inside, Emilio Santoro, tomorrow, and as soon as possible after that I will arrange for your guide.''

"How does the guide know where the base is?" Manning asked.

"Apparently he has delivered supplies to the place on a number of occasions. Sometimes only pack animals are able to get through the rain forest. It is still very primitive country north of Manaus. Not many roads. This is why Mohn has built his base there—the isolation, remoteness." Farrango paused. "One thing I must tell you about Jorgio Cavantes, my informer. He has been known to use drugs. Sometimes cocaine. I believe he receives some of his payments from Mohn in drugs. I realize this places you in a difficult position—having to depend on such a person. I am not happy about it, either. If there was any other way of locating Mohn's base I would use it, believe me."

"Thanks for being honest, Lieutenant Farrango," Manning said. "It's not how we'd like it, but as you say, we can't choose our allies sometimes."

"At least we are aware now," Katz said.

"Just one thing," Farrango added.

"Yes?"

"Please drop the title. Call me Louis."

As they approached the city, Farrango pointed out places of interest and gave them some details of its history. Manaus had originally been established in the seventeenth century as a garrison post and mission at the confluence of the mighty Amazon and the Rio Negro. At the turn of the twentieth century, during the great rubber boom, the city expanded. In those heady years great, opulent buildings were constructed, many of them still standing and vying for space with the newer high rises of present-day Manaus. In 1910 the opera house was completed, where Jenny Lind once sang and the Ballet Russe danced. Decorated with French ironwork and hung with works of art, the opera house appeared to be out of context in its savage jungle surroundings. But such contrasts were a feature of Manaus, a bustling, modern city of nearly one million people, set in the middle of the Amazon jungle. The freewheeling days of the rubber boom ended when the development of rubber plantations in Malaysia destroyed Brazil's monopoly. After a period of dormant years the city took on new life and grew to be a busy tax-free port that was served by oceangoing vessels. It was said to be the nation's smuggling capital.

Farrango drove Katz and Manning along a route that took in the port area, showing them the huge floating dock constructed to handle the river's yearly forty-foot rise and fall. Alongside the dock stood the combination customhouse and lighthouse, which had been imported in pieces from England then reassembled on-site.

As he pulled in at the ten-story Amazonas Hotel, Farrango said, "I will contact you the moment I have confirmation that your friends have arrived. And also the minute I have information that we can go ahead. In the meantime, enjoy your stay in Manaus." He climbed out of the Mercedes and removed the luggage from the trunk, handing it to the smiling bellboy who emerged from the hotel. Katz paid Farrango for the ride, then followed Manning into the hotel. The Phoenix pair registered and were shown to their rooms on the ninth floor, Manning's directly across the hall from Katz's.

As soon as the bellboy had gone Manning joined Katz in his room. The Israeli was standing at the window, gazing out across the city. Beyond the city limits could be seen the hazy spread of the vast Amazon rain forest. In the far distance the green of the forest merged with the purple swell of low mountains, which in turn were lost in the curve of the sky. Over it all seemed to hang a pale, semitransparent mist.

"Beautiful country," Manning said.

Katz nodded. "Yes. It's only the people who spoil it. The ones who want to cut down all the forest, or carve roads through it. Or those who want to dominate the country and tell the people how they should live—not ask them, *tell* them."

"Only if we let them, Yakov. Only if we let them."

Katz sighed a little wearily. "I sometimes think we're swimming against the tide, Gary. So many of them, so few of us. Every time we eliminate one group, two more appear."

"You know what Mack would say. All we can do is our best. Let the savages know some of us *won't* sit back and let it happen."

"I suppose you're right." Katz grinned suddenly. "I must be suffering from jet lag. I need a bath and a change of clothes."

"Sounds good to me," Manning replied.

4

After a day and a half of enjoying the sights and sounds of Manaus, the separated members of Phoenix Force received the message from Louis Farrango that the mission was on. The Brazilian policeman arranged for the Phoenix warriors to come together at the safehouse on the outskirts of the city after darkness had fallen.

Katz and Gary Manning left their taxi on the corner of the street as Farrango had requested, then walked until they spotted the white-painted wood-frame house. At their knock Farrango himself opened the door and they went in.

The interior was neatly decorated and comfortably furnished. In the lounge Farrango showed Katz and Manning to were the other three members of Phoenix Force.

"Better late than never," David McCarter remarked as Katz and Manning entered the room. The British commando was dressed in a rumpled, baggy white suit. He even wore white shoes. Manning grinned from ear to ear. "Who the hell do you think you are? Last time I saw a suit like that was in an old black-and-white movie on television.''

''You know what they say,'' McCarter replied. ''If you wait long enough everything comes back into fashion.''

''Well, you sure didn't wait long enough with that one,'' Calvin James said.

''What have you got to tell us, Louis?'' Katz asked, ignoring the banter; he was used to it, aware that it was a means by which the Phoenix warriors released the tension that built up before a mission got under way.

''Earlier today I received a short Morse code message from my undercover man at Mohn's base,'' Farrango said. ''Emilio was positive that his cover had been broken and that he would not be making contact again. Before he broke off he confirmed that Mohn is in the final stages of preparing some elaborate scheme. There was nothing else.''

''This leaves your man in great danger,'' Katz said. Farrango nodded.

''Have you known Emilio long?'' James asked.

''For many years. We joined the force together, trained together and were partners on the street for almost three years. Emilio showed a talent for undercover work and he joined me when I took on the special squad. He spent six months as a drug processor before Mohn recruited him for work at his secret base. Emilio went in knowing there was no way of smuggling in any form of communicator. My monitoring team worked around the clock for almost three weeks before Emilio came through. We had decided on a short identification code he could use on any kind of transmitter. One evening, very late, the identification code came through in Morse. After that Emilio sent us irregular messages, relaying short items of information. Very slowly I began to build my case against Mohn—until the block was put on. The rest you know."

"Sounds like you have a good man in Emilio," James said.

"And a bloody brave one," McCarter added.

"Emilio knew the risks," Farrango said, "and accepted them . . . but . . ."

"Louis, I wish there was something we could do," Katz said.

Farrango nodded. He saw the concern on the faces of Phoenix Force and realized they did care—because they were men like Emilio and himself, dedicated individuals fighting a ceaseless war against evil in all its forms. Placing themselves willingly on the firing line with total disregard for their own safety.

"Damn!" Gary Manning snapped. "It makes me angry to think of a good man with his back to the wall, and we can't do a thing to help him."

"I thank you all for your concern," Farrango said.

"There is one thing we can do," Encizo said. "If Emilio has sacrificed himself for this operation, then *we* make sure that sacrifice isn't wasted."

"Damn right," Calvin James agreed.

"Then we go ahead," Katz said.

"But surely you must realize the mission is in jeopardy now," Farrango pointed out. "If Emilio's cover has been broken, it is possible there may have been other leaks. Mohn's forces may be waiting for you."

"We understand that," Katz said, "and we accept it as part of the mission."

"And still you will go ahead?"

"We have no other option," Katz explained. "Our brief was to penetrate Mohn's organization and find out what he's up to. If this secret operation presents some kind of threat to the U.S. and the free world, then we have to confront and eliminate it."

"Every mission we accept has its unknown quantity," Manning explained. "There are no guarantees that any plan will go by the book. Every one is different."

"We live with that," James added.

"Adds to the fun," McCarter said lightly. "I mean, if you know the thing's going to be by the book—well, it gets bloody boring. Sharpens a man up if he has to walk on the edge."

"Then I will call Cavantes and arrange the rendezvous. It will take us approximately three hours to drive to the place. From there Cavantes will walk you through the forest."

James had started to unpack the "luggage" Farrango had been looking after—aluminum cases that held the team's weapons and ammunition, clothing and other items. Now he glanced up.

"Any idea how long this trip is going to take?" he asked, lifting his M-16 out of the first case he'd opened.

"Two, maybe three days," Farrango said. "It is difficult to be more precise, simply because we do not know the exact distance to the place."

"Nothing from Emilio?"

Farrango shook his head. "Emilio, like everyone who works at the base, was transported there at night, in a blacked-out helicopter. Mohn will not allow anyone to leave the base, with the exception of a select few of his most trusted aides and his helicopter pilots. Those on the base have no idea where they are."

"I thought your informer, Cavantes, knew the location," Katz said.

"He does. Cavantes is a very curious man, and he took it on himself to find out," Farrango explained. "When he delivers supplies for Mohn, he meets some of Mohn's people at a prearranged place. They take the supplies Cavantes has brought in by mule and load them into a small truck, which then drives off into the forest. On one occasion, taking advantage of a sudden downpour of rain, Cavantes followed the truck. It was not difficult. A single man can easily conceal himself in the forest and still be able to observe a slow-moving truck. Cavantes followed the truck for about ten miles—until it reached the place that was undoubtedly Mohn's base. But he was unable to point out the location on a map. Not that we really have any maps that can be described as topographically correct for that area. The forest is too dense to chart properly.''

"Then we will have to depend on his skills as a guide," Katz said.

"Not forgetting the guy is a doper," McCarter reminded everyone with his usual lack of subtlety.

"I hadn't forgotten, Mr. Forbes," Katz replied stiffly, referring to the British commando by his cover name. "And I'm sure that if I had, you would have kindly reminded me."

"Too true, old chum," McCarter said with a grin, noisily unwrapping a new magazine for his MAC-10.

"How long do you need to get ready?" Farrango asked.

"Couple of hours should do it," James said.

"Then we will leave around five," the Brazilian policeman said.

"That should get us to the rendezvous around dawn."

"Fine," Katz said.

"If you require food or drink, there is a fully stocked kitchen through that door."

When Farrango left, the Phoenix warriors laid out the weapons and equipment they were going to take with them. Every gun was stripped down and checked, each magazine individually loaded. Spare magazines for each gun were prepared and slipped into pouches on the combat harness.

With his Ingram checked to his satisfaction, David McCarter looked to his Browning Hi-Power. He was carrying a new knife, too, on this trip, which he had picked up from the Stony Man arsenal and had tested himself. It was a Gerber Predator CS, a nine-inch, high carbon stainless-steel blade in a bowie design. The superbly balanced knife had a DuPont Hypalon handle that had been redesigned to give maximum grip. McCarter had liked the feel of the weapon the moment he had closed his fingers over the handle.

Calvin James still carried his favorite G96 Boot 'n' Belt knife. It nestled snugly in its sheath at his waist as he clicked a 30-round magazine into his M-16. He laid the rifle down so he could load his Colt Commander with its 7-round magazine of .45 manstoppers.

Along with his FN-FAL assault rifle and his .357 Magnum Desert Eagle, Gary Manning had brought one of the Enfield SA80s. The Canadian had been so impressed by the new weapon's performance that he wanted to put it through some combat trials.

Rafael Encizo had watched Manning put the SA80 through its paces and had been impressed himself by its performance. Even so, he still carried his Heckler & Koch MP-5. The SMG with its 30-round magazine was a tried-and-trusted weapon as far as he was concerned. So was his 9 mm Smith & Wesson handgun.

Katz was well satisfied with his Uzi. The 9 mm SMG had got him out of more tight corners than he cared to recall, as had his SIG-Sauer P-226 autoloader. The Phoenix Force commander had decided he was too set in his ways to start changing weapons.

Each Phoenix pro also carried a selection of fragmentation and concussion grenades, clipped to his harness. Each would also take a backpack that held a change of clothing, combat rations and medical supplies. As soon as they had completed the checking of their weapons, changed into jungle camouflage gear and filled their backpacks, the five warriors made their way to the kitchen.

While James and Encizo prepared food and coffee, Katz sat at the table and passed around the signal devices Jack Grimaldi had given them.

McCarter, in a happy mood because he had discovered a stock of Coca-Cola in the refrigerator, picked up his device and examined it carefully.

"I just hope Jack remembered to put the bloody batteries in," he said.

"Funny," James said.

"It won't be, old mate, if the things are flat." The cockney grinned.

"That's a dream of mine," Manning said to McCarter.

"What is?" asked the Brit.

"That one day *your* damn batteries will go flat," the Canadian said.

"You can be hard sometimes," McCarter told him. Manning just sat there grinning.

The door opened and Farrango came in. He nodded in Katz's direction. "I have spoken to Cavantes. He will be at the rendezvous to meet us. My friends, the mission is set to go."

5

"On your feet! *Schnell! Schnell!*"

The hoarse bellow of the guard standing in the open doorway of his cell dragged Emilio Santoro from his stupor. He groped his way to full consciousness, blinking his eyes against the harsh glare of the powerful lamp set in the ceiling of the cell.

As awareness returned, the pain began to flood back—the keen stabbing in his left side, indicating a cracked or even broken rib, the dull, nagging aches in half a dozen places on his torso, which sharpened to an agonizing pitch when he moved. His head throbbed, while his face felt numb and oddly swollen out of shape. His mouth was parched, and sour with the taste of blood. He felt utterly weary, his body drained, and he knew this was the way they wanted him to feel.

It was all part of the treatment: the savage beating after Mohn's security men had burst into his room and dragged him, protesting, to the cell; the relentless barrage of questions and accusations, yells and screams. The physical and mental abuse had rained down on him for what seemed an eternity. It was in-

tended to break his spirit, his will to resist. They were
determined to do whatever was necessary to get him to
talk—to impart the information they wanted.

But Emilio Santoro had not given them what they
wanted!

His stubborn refusal to talk had infuriated his tor-
mentors and had driven Mohn himself into a frenzy.
The leader of the Nazi group had a pathological hatred
for anyone who dared oppose him. He believed he existed on a higher plane than those around him, and
that his inferiors must never be allowed to go against
his will. In fact, Mohn exemplified the classic Nazi
mentality, which supposed that anyone *not* a Nazi was
some kind of degenerate moron, a subspecies that
must be defiled and broken, trampled on and treated
with the utmost contempt. Kurt Mohn viewed the entire world in that way. He was driven by an inbred assumption that the Nazi way was the only cure for a
sick world.

The problem was, Santoro saw, that the Nazi cure
tended to be all-consuming. Once the jackboots
started marching they kept right on going, and there
were no exceptions. Mohn was already suffering from
the world-domination syndrome, and it showed no
sign of easing off.

The guard who had shouted at Santoro stepped
aside to allow a tall, blond-haired man to enter the
cell.

Kurt Mohn stood well over six feet tall. His powerful body, erect and supple, was clad in a black uni-

form. His face was angular, with a wide mouth and cold blue eyes. He addressed Santoro.

"Refusing to talk, Santoro, will not keep you alive any longer," the Nazi leader said. "I admit it would be interesting to have the information stored in that devious brain of yours, but without it I shall still survive."

"Then why bother me?" The prisoner's dry bruised mouth formed words with great difficulty. "I was trying to relax."

"In your position, Santoro, humor is the last thing that should be on your mind."

"You think so? For God's sake, man, this whole setup is one big laugh. Here you are, buried in the depths of the jungle, miles from anywhere, all dressed up in your fancy uniforms. For what, Mohn? Tell me, because I am very interested."

"Why should I waste my breath explaining to scum like you?" Mohn snapped. "A filthy interloper here only to try to learn what I am doing, and then to betray me!" Mohn snapped his fingers at the guard by the door.

Santoro watched the armed man approach. He thought his final moment had come. Since his capture he had accepted that his final reward from Mohn would be death. The Nazi leader wasn't going to let him go free. Sooner or later, Santoro knew, Mohn would have him put down like a stray dog.

"Bring him," Mohn said to the guard. "As he is so curious about my work here, we shall let him see for himself. Why explain? He can experience it himself, firsthand.''

The grinning guard reached out and caught hold of Santoro's shirt, dragging him to his feet. The undercover policeman swayed unsteadily. The guard planted a big hand in Santoro's back and shoved him toward the open door and the hallway beyond.

Mohn led the way along the corridor. A steel door opened to reveal iron steps leading to the lower level of the building. As they descended the steps, Santoro had to grip the rail tightly to stay upright. He felt dizzy and nauseated. The sick feeling had been bad enough lying down. It was worse now that he was on his feet.

For some reason he began to think about his early days as a policeman, when he and Farrango were working together. They'd been some team. Eager. Dedicated. Intent on putting the world to rights. Those naive dreams had soon been shattered after they'd worked a few months in the roughest part of the city, confronted the day-to-day reality of police work. The violence and the suffering. The depths to which the human spirit could sink. The greed, poverty and despair. And, of course, the great leveler—death. The two young cops had never dreamed there were so many ways to die, so many ways for the human body to be destroyed by another human being. Burned. Strangled. Slashed to death with a knife or a broken bottle, or shot. Dumped in the river and not found for a week or so. In the end a dead body became not a person but a thing. Farrango and Santoro learned to accept. It didn't mean they were indifferent—they had simply adjusted to the work. That meant looking at a ravaged corpse with a cop's eyes and not those of a beginner.

The guard prodded Santoro in the back with the muzzle of his SMG. For a split second Santoro felt the urge to whirl around and smash at the man's face with his clenched fists. It would have been worth it just to see the expression on the guy's face. But of course he didn't try it. It was all he could do to stay on his feet.

They seemed to have walked for miles. Santoro could feel his body shutting down, rebelling against the damage inflicted during the beatings. As he staggered along, his thoughts drifted again.

He was beginning his undercover career, starting the slow process of establishing himself in a down-and-out area of the city so he could get the goods on a dope merchant who had been supplying dirty drugs to the local teenagers. Some kids had died, others were in hospitals where they would probably stay for the rest of their lives. Both Farrango and Santoro had visited those kids in institutions, and they had been stunned at what they saw. Healthy, active teenagers were reduced to pitiful, shambling wrecks: bodies wasted and disease-ridden, minds ruined, eyes once bright and full of hope turned dull and listless. A once-beautiful eighteen-year-old girl had stared at Santoro out of a face that had visited hell and was now a wrinkled mask of despair.

The images of those young victims had stayed with Santoro, visiting him more than once during restless nights. He had burned with anger at the thought of all those lives destroyed forever, and all because of the greed of men. Men who traded the filth called dope. Whether it was cocaine, or heroin, or sugar-coated with the current hip name—speed, crack, smack, snow—it all meant the same thing at the end of the line. Misery and suffering for the users. Hard cash, in millions, for the suppliers. Santoro's anger had grown, a raging fire that drove him on. He became totally dedicated to the eradication of the dope merchants: the growers, the processors, the distributors, the peddlers on street corners who handed out addictive poison to kids eight and nine years old as they came out of school. He wanted them all. He wanted them dead and buried. The cold hard fact that this would never happen was pushed aside. Santoro knew he had to try. Even though the battle was never-ending, victory always out of reach. He had to make the effort. He had to take at least some of them out, to show that somebody cared enough to try.

"In here." Mohn's voice broke through Santoro's thoughts, dragging him back to reality. To the cold, stark truth of his situation. "Open the door."

With a soft hiss a door slid open. The guard behind Santoro stepped in close. He put a brutal hand between Santoro's shoulders and shoved hard, propelling the undercover cop forward through the open door and into the room beyond. Before he could recover his balance Santoro heard the door hiss again, and as he turned he saw it lock shut, with a hard thump.

Santoro straightened and took a look around. The room he was in appeared to be constructed out of white metal. It reminded him of an operating room. He shivered as the thought struck him. There was no furniture. No shelves on the walls. The place was not designed for living in, or for any long-term occupancy.

A soft electric hum caught Santoro's attention. He turned toward it. In the wall behind him a panel slid aside to reveal a large window. Beyond the window stood Mohn, watching him, a thin smile on his taut face. A man appeared at Mohn's side. He was tall and thin, almost skeletal, his long face deeply pock-marked from some ravaging disease. He spoke to Mohn. Santoro saw the man's lips moving, but heard nothing. He was in a completely soundproofed chamber.

What were Mohn and the other man up to? Santoro wondered, and felt the first faint flickerings of anxiety. They had something planned for him, and there was no way it was going to be pleasant. Mohn leaned forward and touched something below the level of the window. A moment later his voice rang through the room with a metallic resonance.

"An interesting room, Santoro. You may have noticed that it is completely soundproof. It is also airtight. Entirely self-contained."

Santoro's anxiety became fear. The feeling grew, fed upon itself as it engulfed Santoro's body. Fear of the unknown. Of something utterly alien.

Santoro's physical weakness neutralized his ability to resist the fear, leaving the way open for Mohn's words to implant themselves on his defenseless mind.

"Listen, Santoro," Mohn said. *"Listen!"*

The room was filled with a swelling hiss.

Santoro turned, seeking the source of the sound. It came from somewhere over his head. Then he spotted the small square opening in the ceiling, no more than a couple of inches across. Just visible inside the recess was a gleaming metal nozzle. The hissing sound came from the nozzle.

Something was being pumped into the room. Gas!

They were going to poison him! But he smelled nothing, tasted nothing in the air.

Beyond the window Mohn and his assistant regarded him with amused curiosity. They were conversing, but once again they could not be heard, and Santoro could not read their lips.

The hissing stopped. The opening in the ceiling vanished as a panel closed over the now silent nozzle.

A minute passed. Another.

Santoro retreated to the far side of the white room and squatted at the base of the wall, his gaze fixed on Mohn. His panic had subsided a little. He was still frightened, and would have readily admitted the fact, but some degree of control had returned to him. Santoro knew now that he was not going to get out of the room alive, and he found himself accepting the fact with surprising calm. If anything, he felt sadness, because as he died, so would the will and energy he had been channeling into his battle against the evil of drugs. His death would be little noticed in the world at large, and the pain and suffering of all those innocents caught up in the drug spiral would go on as if he had never existed.

He scratched the back of his left hand. The flesh was tingling. The sensation extended along his arm. The more he scratched, the worse the irritation became. It broke out across the back of his neck, swept across his chest beneath his shirt.

As Santoro began to rub furiously at his body he became aware of a heaviness in his hands. He glanced down at them. The flesh on his hands was puckering; it bulged and dipped as if living things were moving beneath the surface. His head began to ache, not as before, from the beating, but as if a band of steel was being tightened around his skull. His nausea worsened, and he began to heave uncontrollably, the vomit spilling from him in a torrent. Even when there was nothing left to bring up, he continued to retch, each convulsion of his stomach bringing a burning pain.

He noticed that the flesh of his hands was discolored. Bulging pustules rose. The joints of his fingers stiffened as the tissue around them filled out, ballooning grotesquely. Now he could feel his face become distorted, his mouth twisted, the glands in his neck swelling. Breathing became difficult. His tongue felt too large for his mouth. He tried to climb to his feet, but found his coordination slipping away. Half standing, he stumbled sideways, slithering along the wall. He fell, struggled upright again and somehow managed to find his feet. Awkwardly he lurched across the room until he was able to lean his tortured body against the soundproof window and stare through it at Mohn.

The man's eyes held nothing but cold, unfeeling contempt. Mohn simply glanced at Santoro once, then turned to talk animatedly to the man beside him. The thin man had a watch in his hand, which he glanced at every now and then while he made notes on a large clipboard he carried.

Santoro felt his awareness fading rapidly. His body was a mass of irritation now, its surface crawling, inflamed. He felt as if he were being eaten alive by millions of creeping insects that had burrowed beneath his flesh. Many of the swollen pustules on his hands and arms had burst, spilling yellow-green pus over his skin. The smarting grew more intense, and Santoro pulled at his clothing in an attempt to scratch, but all he managed to do was to burst more of the pustules. He clawed at his face, tearing the flesh. Blood mingled with the pus from the festering sores.

Santoro slipped to the floor without being aware of it. He was nearly unconscious, his mind and body retreating from the relentless advance of the disease claiming him. He lay, eyes open, staring at the ceiling of the room but not seeing it, not even registering anymore where he was. His ravaged body quivered in feeble protest as the nerve ends registered the final attack. Santoro's chest began to rise and fall rapidly, his mouth opening as he struggled for breath. Saliva drooled from his lips. His body arched from the floor in a last desperate attempt to draw air into his starved lungs. The attempt failed. Santoro flopped back to the floor, his form taking on that curious limpness only the dead acquire.

On the opposite side of the soundproof window Kurt Mohn turned to his companion. "Well?"

The pockmarked man glanced at his watch, nodding in a pleased fashion. "It is good," he said. He spoke in a low whisper, his words delivered in a heavy German accent. "Two minutes precisely. At least thirty-five seconds off the previous sample."

Mohn smiled. "I think this is the one, Otto. Have the laboratory start work on producing sufficient quantities. It must be ready within a week."

The man called Otto looked up from his clipboard, doubt on his face. "A week is—" he began.

"Is what you have, Otto," Mohn said evenly. There was ice in his tone, and a bleak expression in his eyes.

Otto Neiman nodded acknowledgement. He knew his place and meant to keep it. Even if it meant doing the impossible. He had learned from the mistakes of others, and had seen what could happen to those foolish enough to question Kurt Mohn's judgment. One look at the shriveled remains of the police undercover man, Emilio Santoro, was enough to convince

Neiman that he could and would produce what Mohn had asked for. And in the specified period of time.

"What of the specialists brought in by the president?" he asked.

Mohn turned away from the window of the death chamber and began to retrace his steps along the corridor, with Neiman at his side. "That is being handled," he said. "Cavantes is playing his part well. The policeman, Farrango, believes Cavantes is still working for him. The American specialists will be guided into the jungle by Cavantes, and at the prearranged place and time will be delivered into the hands of our waiting force."

"And then their lives will be in *our* hands," Neiman mused, pleased at the prospect.

"If any survive, of course," Mohn said. "I expect they will put up a fight. It will provide our force with some field experience." He paused in midstride. "Otto, do not forget to have Santoro's body removed and incinerated immediately. We cannot afford any more accidents."

Mohn continued along the corridor, his mind preoccupied with matters more urgent than the disposal of one dead undercover policeman.

6

"One thing I'd like to emphasize, Louis," Katz said as the Volkswagen minibus rolled along the bumpy back road.

Farrango briefly took his eyes from the dusty track and glanced at the Phoenix warrior. "Yes?"

"The backup helicopter. We want it to be our secret. Say nothing about it to Cavantes. It's our insurance. If we need to abort the mission, or if we get into difficulties, that chopper is the only way we can get out."

"So mum's the word," McCarter chimed in breezily. "We trust *you*, Louis, but everybody else should be on a need-to-know basis."

"I can't blame you for that," Farrango said. "After all, my own man has been caught out. Security appears to be a little shaky."

"Hey, don't worry about it, man," Calvin James said. "Keeping total security is one of the hardest things to do."

"At the end of the day you're trusting in people," Encizo pointed out, "and people are the most unpredictable factors in any game."

Morning was beginning to lighten the sky, pushing back the darkness. They had left the safehouse in the predawn hush, loading their equipment into the back of the minibus while it was still in the garage next to the house. When it was time to move off, the men of Phoenix Force had entered the garage to take seats in the Volkswagen. Farrango had opened the garage doors, driven the vehicle outside, then returned to close those doors. He had driven away from the city using quiet secondary roads. Once clear of Manaus, he chose a rutted dirt road that cut its way through the rain forest. On either side lay the dense thickets of the forest itself, always encroaching on the man-made road.

The deserted road enabled the Phoenix Force members to check their equipment a final time before strapping it on.

"I read somewhere that vast areas of this forest are being stripped of timber by logging companies," Manning remarked. "It said if the cutting goes on at the present rate, large tracts of forest will be destroyed."

"That is true," Farrango said. "And not only the trees are vanishing. So much plant and animal life in the forests is being lost, too. These forests are the breeding ground for hundreds of plants and living things that have yet even to be discovered and named. If the destruction continues many of these species will vanish before anyone has the chance to study or even photograph them."

"Can't anyone stop it?" Encizo asked.

"No," Farrango said. "There is too much money being made. And money is power."

"Same old story," McCarter said. "Wave big bucks in people's faces and ethics get kicked out the door."

"When you think about it," Manning said, "we all live in the same kind of world. America. Europe. Brazil. 'Money is power' is the theme of the whole show."

McCarter leaned across and tapped Manning's shoulder. "I hate it when you go all cynical. You're no fun then."

The sky grew lighter as the sun rose overhead. Then clouds drifted over and rain fell. At first the drops kicked up puffs of dry dust as they hit the ground, but soon the downpour turned the dust to mud. The rain fell for at least half an hour, then stopped as quickly as it had started. The clouds drifted away and a warm sun shone out of the streaked sky.

"These short periods of rain sometimes happen two or three times a day," Farrango explained. "In the forest frequent rain and high temperatures create a very humid atmosphere. The canopy of the forest overhead traps the heat and makes it like a steam bath at ground level."

"I like it hot," McCarter muttered.

"He means sweaty hot," Encizo told the Briton. "Not bullet hot."

"All the same to me." The ex-SAS ace grinned.

Encizo didn't reply, figuring it was no use. The British commando always seemed to get the last word, as relentless with his sarcasm and wit as he was with a weapon.

They saw no other traffic on the whole trip. The dusty track stretched out before them, devoid of human life. As the hours dragged by even the spontaneous kidding between McCarter and Manning dried up, and the men settled back to relax as best they could, conserving their energy for what lay ahead.

Katz reached into his pocket to touch the signal device Jack Grimaldi had given to each member of Phoenix Force. Katz's unit was activated at present, sending out its signal to Dragon Slayer. Somewhere behind them, high in the empty sky, Grimaldi was following the electronic marker. He would stay out of sight, but if the team needed him, the signal device would lead him to them quickly. That was the theory, anyway. But Katz had lived long enough to know that the cavalry didn't always come thundering over the hill at exactly the right moment—which Custer had found out, to his cost. The Israeli contented himself with the knowledge that they were at least going in with as much preplanning as was feasible. In the end, as usual, they would have to depend mainly on their own experience and instinct.

Farrango brought the minibus to a stop at the side of the track and killed the engine. "About a mile and a half farther along is a small settlement. It used to belong to a rubber company many years ago, but when the rubber business folded, the place was abandoned. It was taken over by smugglers, criminals, you name it. It stands on the bank of the Rio Negro. Cavantes hangs out there, and most of the people in the place are his cronies. None of them are to be trusted. I'm going to drive a little farther, then park about a mile from the settlement. I'll go to meet Cavantes, then bring him back to you people. I'm known to his friends as a dealer in illicit goods. They haven't accepted me fully, but that doesn't matter—they tolerate me. After Cavantes goes off with you, I'll hang around the settlement. The main building, which is used as a trading post, has rooms in the back. I'll take one of those, and stay there until I hear from you."

Katz nodded. "You watch out for yourself, Louis," he said. "There are too many unknowns in this operation."

"I understand," Farrango said.

The Brazilian policeman started the Volkswagen again and drove to his prearranged spot. Then he left the van and, with a quick wave to Phoenix Force, walked off along the track, finally vanishing around a bend.

The men of Phoenix Force got out of the minibus, too. They pulled on their backpacks and swiftly checked their equipment.

"Katz," McCarter began, joining the Phoenix commander.

"I know, you still feel uneasy about Cavantes."

"Too bloody right," the Briton answered.

"So you want to keep a close eye on him. Right?"

McCarter grinned. "Too smart, that's your problem, mate."

"I think you're right, David," Katz said. "Do it on the quiet. Don't let him see he's being watched, but stay on his back."

"Consider it done." McCarter wandered off with a pleased smile on his face.

Farrango returned within half an hour, followed closely by a lean brown-skinned man with a thick mass of jet-black hair. Jorgio Cavantes was dressed in grubby olive shirt and pants. He wore leather boots and carried a stained baseball cap in one of his wiry hands. The canvas holster supported by the belt around his waist held a Colt .45 automatic pistol, while in a webbing sling on his shoulder was a Kalashnikov AK-47. A filled canvas bag was slung over his other shoulder, and dangling from a leather thong around his left wrist was a long-bladed machete.

As Farrango made brief introductions, to which Cavantes nodded, David McCarter studied the guide closely. The cockney commando had built-in radar when it came to judging people, and it seldom failed him. Right now the warning lights were flashing. McCarter knew now he had been correct all along. Coming face-to-face with Jorgio Cavantes only confirmed what he had felt from the beginning—the man was going to need very close watching.

McCarter couldn't put a finger on what it was in Cavantes that bothered him. It was just a feeling.

There was something in the way the man spoke, the way he carried himself, and especially in his face. His eyes were too bright, too probing. They held an elusive expression that came and went, never settling for too long on anyone's face, and avoiding prolonged eye contact.

In short, McCarter did not trust the man. He decided the word to describe Cavantes was *shifty*. Or maybe *slippery*.

Cavantes, my friend, you are going under the microscope, McCarter promised silently. And I'm not letting you out of my sight for one bloody minute.

Cavantes spoke briefly to Farrango, then clapped the dirty cap on his head and glanced over his shoulder at Katz. "We go," he announced, and shuffled off.

Phoenix Force followed. Katz walked directly behind Cavantes, with McCarter a few yards to one side. James and Encizo came next, each taking one side of the trail to watch. Gary Manning brought up the rear.

They broke away from the dirt track and moved directly into the forest. Almost immediately the timber and foliage closed in around them. The ground beneath their feet was soft, spongy and moist. The air was humid, rich with the smells of decaying vegetation and luxuriant blooms. Shafts of sunlight lanced down through the canopy formed by the lush growth of leaves high above the forest floor. Thick lianas wound around the tree trunks, reaching up toward the sun and the open air. All around was the ever-present background noise of the forest—the chatter of monkeys swinging back and forth in the high branches, the harsh cackle of birds. In the shadows of the thick undergrowth, unseen creatures rattled and slithered away from the men's crushing boots.

The Amazon jungle was a sweltering hothouse of exotic plants and creatures that oozed moisture from every pore. Plants glistened. The earth underfoot was soggy. Within a quarter of an hour the men were all dripping with sweat. The humid atmosphere sucked the moisture from them. Their clothes clung to their wet bodies. Sweat trickled into their eyes and left salty traces on their lips. Even the weapons they carried became slippery in their damp hands.

"If there's one thing I can't stand," McCarter grumbled, "it's wet socks."

"I've learned something about this place already," James said.

"What?" Encizo asked.

"It really sucks," the black Phoenix commando said, grinning.

Cavantes set a steady pace. He obviously knew this part of the jungle well. He pushed ahead, swinging his machete to great effect, cutting away any obstacle that blocked their path. He spoke only when it was absolutely necessary. The rest of the time he communicated by pointing with his machete to guide them around a deep ravine and show them where to cross a stream or pool. They trudged on, until long after midday.

Katz frequently removed a compass from his pocket to check the direction in which they were travelling. They were moving steadily north. He thought about Grimaldi, wondering if the man still had them on his screen in Dragon Slayer.

It was almost two o'clock when Cavantes called a halt. He cleared himself a spot at the base of a tree and squatted on his heels. After pulling a canteen from his canvas bag, he took a swallow of water. "Rest," he said. "Ten minutes."

"Regular little hardass," James muttered as he unclipped his canteen and sipped a mouthful of tepid water.

McCarter wiped sweat from his face with his sleeve. "He's asking for my boot up his arse—hard or not."

As the teammates took advantage of the opportunity to relax briefly, large drops of rain spattered onto the foliage around them. Within a minute of their noticing the first drops, they were in a downpour. The rain rattled against the tough leaves, collecting in pools on the sodden ground.

Phoenix Force remained where they were, taking their rest. There was nowhere for them to hide from the torrential rain, for the jungle around them offered nothing in the way of protection. They were so damp already from sweat and the humidity, a little more seemed of no consequence.

It was still raining when Cavantes got to his feet and announced once again, "We go."

The members of Phoenix Force climbed to their feet and followed the weaving figure of the guide as he hacked his own path through the drenched undergrowth. For the next four hours they trekked north but when Katz checked his compass just before Cavantes called a halt for the night, he saw that they had angled slightly west.

The guide had brought them to an area where the thick forest gave way to a series of rocky ravines. One by one they made their way down to the floor of one of the defiles, Cavantes leading them to a shallow cave set in a solid wall of rock. The jutting overhang of the cave provided a natural roof, protecting them from any more rain.

Without a word to the others Cavantes gathered some of the dried wood scattered around the cave and took it to a blackened area on the ground, where fires had obviously been lit before. Deftly Cavantes arranged the wood and got a fire going. He took a blackened coffeepot from his canvas bag and filled it from a stream that ran across the frontage of the cave area. When the water got hot over the fire, he produced crushed coffee beans from a rolled cloth bag and scattered them in the steaming water.

Calvin James, who, like his teammates, was drying his weapons, watched Cavantes. "That guy would make someone a good wife," he remarked.

"They said the same thing about Lucrezia Borgia," McCarter said sarcastically.

Cavantes took his own food from the bag, declining the tinned rations offered to him by Katz.

"Maybe he doesn't trust us," Encizo said softly.

McCarter grinned like a wolf anticipating a kill. "He isn't as dumb as he looks."

When the coffee was ready Cavantes filled his battered tin mug, then brought the pot over to where the others were gathered, left it there and returned to his own solitary spot.

Manning picked up the pot and filled five mugs.

"Do you think Jack is still with us?" James asked.

"He'll be up there," McCarter said. "All wrapped up snug and warm in his bloody cabin. Wouldn't surprise me if he's got a video player in among all that hardware. Probably sitting with his feet up watching a blue movie."

"Trouble with you," Manning said, "is you believe everyone is as perverted as you are."

McCarter looked surprised. "You mean they're not?"

Katz drained his mug. "Let's turn in. It'll be a long day tomorrow. I want you all on your toes, just in case."

"Who's on first watch?" Encizo asked.

The matter hadn't been discussed previously, yet each Phoenix man had understood the need to cover themselves against any surprise move, which meant maintaining a night watch.

"I'll take the first one," James said.

Katz nodded. "All right. Two hours each should see us through. I'll take over from Calvin. Rafael next. Then David. Gary, you take the tail end."

James picked up his M-16 and settled himself with his back to the rock wall, where he could see the approach to the cave. The rest of the team settled down to sleep, each wondering what surprises the new day would hold for them.

7

It was midmorning of the third day out. Following Cavantes, Phoenix Force was still moving north northwest. The day was oppressively humid, and the general mood was of restrained tension.

Jorgio Cavantes's only verbal communication that morning had been to express the news that they were getting close. It was hardly an improvement on the previous day's conversation.

McCarter was still making a point of observing Cavantes closely. From the moment he had set eyes on the man that morning, he had noticed a subtle change in Cavantes's manner. The guide seemed to have become nervous about something. The signs were slight and would easily have been missed by a casual observer. McCarter was far from casual.

His unobtrusive observation of Cavantes had given him enough insight into the man's character to be able to predict more or less how the man might react in a given situation. During the long trek of the previous day he had tested his theory a number of times and had been well satisfied with the results. It proved, if nothing else, that Jorgio Cavantes was a predictable man. It was that predictability that allowed McCarter to anticipate the moment when Cavantes the guide became Cavantes the betrayer.

McCarter had observed Cavantes as he carried out several casual adjustments to his belongings. First, he had pulled on the tie cord of the bag holding his supplies, drawing the bag close to his body. Minutes later he had dropped a hand to his holstered Colt and drawn into place the leather strap that held the weapon secure in the holster. None of these actions had been performed before. Then the machete, which had lived in Cavantes's right hand as he had hacked his way thought thick undergrowth, was passed to his left hand, the AK-47 to his right.

Seeing these individual acts in isolation would have meant little. But McCarter's close watch on Cavantes made him aware that the guide had not carried out any of these maneuvers before. To perform them all within a relatively short space of time had to indicate something.

McCarter deduced that Cavantes's reason for these actions might well be that he was anticipating a sudden move—securing his bag so it wouldn't get in his way, tying down his handgun to keep it from jumping from the holster, transferring his rifle to his right hand because he was considering having to use it.

Having reasoned out an acceptable cause for the actions, McCarter was still paying particular attention to the guide's movements, when they broke from the relatively thick forest and began to cross a clearing that was sprinkled with only a few trees. Halfway across, Cavantes threw a quick glance over his shoulder, then peered off to his left, to where the forest lay dense and seemingly deserted. Looking in the same direction, McCarter's keen eyes caught a fragmentary flash of pale sunlight glancing off metal deep within the foliage.

At that same moment Cavantes turned abruptly, lunging for the cover of the forest.

I knew it, McCarter thought. The bugger's walked us into a trap! To his Phoenix teammates he yelled a warning. "Scatter! Bloody move it! Ambush!"

The command motivated Phoenix Force into concerted action, action that came just ahead of the first enemy shot. Seconds later the forest echoed with the blast of autofire, and the Phoenix mission suddenly went hard.

KATZ, JAMES AND MANNING, stripped of their weapons, were being herded through the rain forest, their captors moving them at a steady pace.

Overhead they heard the clatter of rotors. An Mi-24 Hind-D gunship came swinging in over the treetops, dropping toward the clearing toward which the Phoenix warriors were being directed. The Russian-built helicopter, painted in camouflage drab, sported a 12.7 mm, four-barrel rotary cannon in an undernose turret and UV-32 rocket pods beneath the stub wings.

"At least we don't have to walk," James said.

"I think I'd prefer to walk," Manning remarked.

The leader of the attack force prodded Manning with the muzzle of his AK-47. "No talking," he ordered.

Manning glanced at him, his expression full of contempt. "Where's your authority?" he asked.

The blond man smiled, then delivered a sharp blow to Manning's jaw with the butt of his AK-47. The burly Canadian stumbled back and would have fallen if James hadn't caught hold of him.

"No talking," the man repeated. He raised a hand and indicated the helicopter which by then had landed. "Get them on board," he ordered his companions. "Don't forget the blindfolds."

As the Phoenix commandos were bundled into the Hind the blond man gestured to one of his men. "Take four men and search for the two who went into the water. I want confirmation they are dead. The helicopter will return for you midmorning tomorrow. Rendezvous here." To another of his squad he said, "Get our dead and wounded on board so we can take off."

As he climbed aboard the Hind the blond man took out of his pocket the three signal devices he had confiscated from the prisoners. He settled in his seat, feeling the Hind surge as the pilot took the machine off the ground. After examining the devices, he placed them on the floor and deliberately crushed them under the heel of his combat boot. Opening a small side window, he tossed the devices out, letting them fall into the green wilderness of the rain forest below.

8

"We've probably caught every disease known to medical science," David McCarter grumbled.

He and Encizo were concealed beneath thick foliage several yards from the pool from which they had recently emerged.

"You're too mean to catch anything," Encizo told his British companion.

"I just hope you're right."

The sound of the Hind's rotors had drifted away and the normal sounds of the forest had returned, accompanied by human noise. A group of men were approaching the area, and not being too quiet about it.

"The cleanup squad," McCarter said. "Coming to check if we're properly dead."

"They'll be disappointed," Encizo remarked.

"Tough shit," McCarter muttered, flicking mud off his cheek.

Encizo began to swear softly in his native tongue.

"Translate, chum," McCarter suggested.

"I was thinking about what I would do if I got my hands on Cavantes."

"Stand in line," McCarter said. "That creep's going to wish he'd never been born when I get to him."

"First things first," Enciso said. "We need to deal with our noisy friends."

McCarter slid his Gerber Predator from its sheath. "They'll quiet down, Rafael. Very soon."

Enciso nodded, drawing his Cold Seal Tanto.

"You take the right flank," McCarter said. "I'll take the left. Come on them from the rear."

The Phoenix warriors slid silently into the forest, circling away from each other, until they were concealed by the deep foliage.

McCarter rose to his feet, easing smoothly through the dense greenery, eyes and ears tuned to pick up the sound of the approaching group.

He paused once, giving himself a few moments to clear his mind for what lay ahead. He could not afford to be distracted by the concerns he had for his captured friends. He needed to ignore these intrusions until this present crisis was over.

But the thoughts—feelings, really—persisted. He was concerned for Katz and James and Manning. His only consolation was that they were still alive, and as long as they were, there was always a chance. There had to be a chance. Phoenix Force deserved better than this. The possibility of being killed or wounded in combat was an acceptable part of the job. But death while in captivity—and in captivity due to betrayal—was no way for any fighting man to die. The reminder about betrayal brought to the fore McCarter's other distracting feeling—the anger he felt against Jorgio Cavantes. If McCarter had allowed it, the anger could easily have overwhelmed him, taken full control of his heart and mind. But that would have been the worst thing he could do. His fears for his Phoenix buddies and his rage against Cavantes, justified as they were, could not be allowed to cloud his thoughts or dictate his actions now.

The first priority now was to deal with the members of the attack force left behind to clean up.

The British warrior flattened himself against the wide trunk of a towering, liana-wrapped tree. Just yards to his right one of the cleanup squad was moving through the foliage. Peering around the far side of the tree, McCarter was able to get a good look at the man. He was more than six feet tall, with pale hair and paler eyes. His combat clothing fit him snugly, as if he were wearing too small a size. He was carrying his M-60 like a handgun, the ammunition belt draped over his shoulder.

McCarter shook his head as he watched the guy tramp by. Another Rambo freak, he thought.

As the M-60 gunner moved ahead, McCarter slid around the tree and came up behind him. The Brit didn't hesitate, but reached up with his left hand, caught hold of the gunner's hair and yanked his head back. In the same instant the razor edge of the Predator whipped across the taut neck. It cut deep and clean, opening the guy's throat. Rich streams of blood bubbled from the severed veins and arteries, and the guy began to choke. He let go of the M-60, clutching both big hands to his gaping neck. Blood spurted between his fingers. As big as he was, the guy couldn't fight the massive blood loss. He stumbled about, colliding with a tree, and sagged to his knees, where he finished bleeding to death.

McCarter moved on, seeking another target, while Encizo dealt with his first. The Cuban's quarry was armed with an AK-47, slung over his shoulder while he pulled a pack of cigars from his pockets and selected one. He put it in his mouth, took out a throwaway lighter and lit up.

Encizo could hardly believe what he was seeing. Here was a so-called combat soldier on a search for a presumed—but unconfirmed—dead enemy. The guy didn't even have the sense to carry his weapon in his hands. He was more concerned with getting a lighted cigar in his mouth.

Checking the area, Encizo saw another member of the attack force up ahead. The man was far enough away from Encizo's chosen target, that if he took out the smoker without too much noise, the man up ahead wouldn't be alerted.

The Phoenix warrior moved silently through the greenery. The moist ground underfoot helped to deaden the sound of his footsteps. Gripping his Tanto, he rose to his full height as he came up behind the cigar smoker. He clapped one hand over the guy's mouth, knocking the cigar to the ground. The other hand drove in the Tanto under the startled man's ribs to pierce the heart. Encizo felt him stiffen in shock. The body convulsed and it took all of Encizo's strength to hold the dying man motionless. As the struggling ceased the Cuban lowered the man to the ground.

But fate decreed that the man up ahead should turn at that moment, his words freezing on his lips as he spotted Encizo. The guy pulled up the drooping barrel of his AK-47 and ripped off a stream of 7.62 mm rounds in Encizo's direction.

The moment he saw the man turn his way, Encizo had made a grab for the Kalashnikov that had slipped from the dead man's shoulder. In a continuation of his move he hit the ground, rolling smoothly away from the corpse. He heard the chatter of the other guy's weapon, heard and felt the whack of the bullets as they chewed the earth around him. Then he was on his stomach, his borrowed weapon finding target acquisition as he aimed by instinct. He touched the trigger and the AK-47 stuttered viciously.

Encizo's volley tore into the other guy's torso, spraying blood and fleshy debris out between his shoulders. As the guy went down, thrashing wildly, his weapon angled skyward, sending a stream of slugs into the green canopy overhead.

Gaining his feet, Encizo snatched a replacement magazine from the guy he'd knifed and shoved it in his pocket. He ran forward, eyes searching the way ahead and to either side. Where were the others? he wondered.

Another AK-47 began to chatter, sending bullets scorching through the foliage. Encizo dropped to the ground, his weapon at the ready. He fired a sustained burst in the direction the previous volley had come from.

The chatter of Encizo's rifle was overridden by the louder thunder of an M-60. A man screamed in pain, then a bullet-shredded form burst from the foliage and crashed to the forest floor only yards from where Encizo lay. The fatally hit enemy twisted and squirmed in agony, clutching bloody hands to his pulped torso. Blood squirted between his fingers, staining the greenery around him. McCarter pushed his way through the foliage, holding the M-60 in his hands. He glanced down at Encizo. "Silly time to take a rest," he said.

Encizo climbed to his feet, ejecting the partly used magazine from the AK-47 and replacing it with the fresh one he'd taken from the dead man.

"There's one more around somewhere," McCarter said. "Let's smoke him out, Rafael, see if we can bring him back alive. Maybe we can squeeze the creep for some information."

Encizo nodded.

The Phoenix pair split again, each taking a different direction. Their intention was to flank the remaining member of the cleanup squad, to draw him into the center of their target area. There was no guarantee the guy would fall in with their scheme. He might have a different idea altogether. If he was aware of his companions' demise, he might have quit the area already, or decided to simply lie down, out of sight, until McCarter and Encizo themselves left.

On the other hand, he could be crazy enough to imagine he could complete the job himself, in which case he might come barreling out of the undergrowth like a charging bull, spraying bullets as he ran.

Which was just what the guy did. He moved fast, with the dedication of a true believer in his cause, whatever that was. His AK-47 was up and firing, 7.62s zipping through the air and causing untold damage to several tree trunks.

The man's sudden appearance caused Encizo a moment of extreme discomfort. But the Phoenix warrior responded instantly, twisting around to face the attack head-on. He found himself directly in the guy's path, with little time to pull his weapon into the firing position. All Encizo could do was duck below the guy's Kalashnikov and throw himself bodily into the man's legs. Encizo hit him hard, slamming him off his feet to dump him on the ground with a bone-jarring crash. Before the guy could recover, Encizo gained his feet. He kicked the AK-47 from the enemy's hands, then rammed the muzzle of his own weapon into the man's throat. There was no need for words. Encizo's warning was clear enough in any language.

"Here," Encizo called. "Over here!"

By the time McCarter appeared, Encizo had the prisoner sitting with his back to a tree, his hands clasped on top of his head.

"Now who's a clever boy," the Brit said dryly as he sauntered across to where Encizo waited. "You sure you really need me?"

"Let me think about it." Encizo grinned. "Now what do we do with laughing boy?"

"Good question," McCarter said. He glanced at the prisoner. "Can you understand me?" he asked.

"Go to hell, Yank," the prisoner said.

"I think he understands," McCarter said. He turned back to the prisoner. "Just one thing, chum. I'm not a Yank, I'm British."

The man glared at McCarter.

"I don't feel he's going to be very helpful," Mc-Carter remarked.

Encizo slid his Tanto from its sheath. "He might change his mind," he said.

McCarter grinned at the prisoner. "If I was you, mate, I'd start being very friendly, because this crazy guy just loves carving people up with that bloody samurai sword."

"I won't tell you anything," the prisoner said, his gaze fixed on the glittering blade in Encizo's hand.

McCarter shrugged. "You please yourself. I was just trying to give you a friendly bit of advice."

Encizo handed his AK-47 to McCarter. He moved toward the prisoner, the Tanto in plain sight.

A faint sheen of perspiration gleamed on the prisoner's face. He pressed close to the tree trunk at his back. Encizo crouched in front of him, the blade of the Tanto carving figure eights in the air.

"Well?" he asked McCarter over his shoulder.

"You go ahead," McCarter said, playing the game.

The prisoner lunged forward, away from the tree. His face was flushed with rage, eyes staring wildly. His powerful frame slammed into Encizo, knocking him off balance. As he struck Encizo, the prisoner twisted toward McCarter, his hands reaching for the Kalashnikov the Briton held in his left hand. He closed his fingers around the weapon, yanked it free and rolled clear. Before either McCarter or Encizo could respond, the prisoner had reversed the AK-47. He shoved the muzzle in his mouth, angling the weapon, and jammed his finger against the trigger. The Kalashnikov's burst of fire blew the top of his skull off in a bloody spray of bone and brains and flesh. Blood spurted from the guy's ears and nose as he toppled over onto his back. His left arm jerked in ugly spasms for a while, stopping soon after the blood had ceased bubbling from the great open wound that had been the top of his head.

"Bugger it!" McCarter said. "We blew that one, Rafael."

"Hell of a drastic way to avoid answering a few questions," the Cuban replied, wiping blood from his cheek with his sleeve. "He was either scared of the knife—"

"—or more scared of giving away Mohn's secrets," McCarter finished.

Encizo stood, putting away his knife. "Let's go pick up our gear, David, and get on our way."

"Cavantes?" McCarter guessed.

Encizo nodded. "Yes, Cavantes."

"First thing we have to do is to get Jack in here," McCarter said. "Right now we need a ride in Dragon Slayer."

9

As he waited and watched for the Hind to arrive at the compound, Kurt Mohn's mind was preoccupied with other matters. For some reason he didn't understand, he was thinking about his father. Joachim Mohn was never completely out of his son's thoughts. Even though he had been dead for almost a year, Joachim Mohn still influenced his offspring. The younger Mohn had been molded by his father from birth, indoctrinated through his life, and so great had been Joachim Mohn's domination of his son, his hold had not been broken by something so insubstantial as death. Kurt Mohn's world centered around the single most important cause in his father's life.

The rebirth of the Third Reich.

That cause had become Joachim Mohn's obsession, his reason for staying alive. When a son was born to him, Mohn saw in him a way of perpetuating that obsession. As Kurt grew, he was immersed in a world that was totally dedicated to nurturing the legends of Hitler's Reich, planted so they could survive until the day of rebirth.

Kurt had embraced the Hitler legacy with open arms, his willingness fueled by his adored father's fanatical loyalty to his goal. Although the Second World War was over, the dream of a Third Reich shattered into a thousand fragments, there were still those who held on to that dream. Living in every corner of the globe, they concealed their Nazi sympathies, always waiting, always hoping.

During those early years following the end of the war, the world had proved to be an inhospitable place for the Hitler fanatics. Many die-hard Nazis, too rigid even to consider change, clung to their beliefs and their allegiance. They were so entrenched in the Nazi ways, there was no way of hiding the fact. In the witch-hunts that followed the end of the war the die-hards were dealt with swiftly.

Others, believing they were too clever to be found out, simply denied any connection with the Nazi party. Even when brought to trial and faced with overwhelming evidence, they clung to their stories. Some, admitting eventually that they might have been involved, used what was to become a historical cliché. *I was only obeying orders.* They believed it to be the magic phrase that would free them. They were wrong, because it had no effect on the war-crimes courts.

Then there were those Nazis who had seen the end coming and had made plans accordingly. They realized that Hitler's great scheme had failed, and that there was a world beyond Germany seeking revenge. Too much had been suffered by too many people, and no amount of pleading for forgiveness would earn a reprieve for those responsible. No silver tongue could erase the horror of what had been done to the wretched innocents of Belsen or Dachau or Auschwitz. The deeds had been done. The time of retribution was at hand.

The wise ones, therefore, chose quiet withdrawal. They packed the bare essentials, gathered their accumulated loot, or Swiss bankbooks, and bought passage on rusty cargo ships heading out across the gray Atlantic. They stood at the rails, clutching their forged passports and identity papers, and watched the verdant coastlines of the South American continent come into view. After disembarking they vanished silently into the remote wildernesses of Brazil, Venezuela, Bolivia and Colombia.

These were the survivors. Men who could adapt, blend into a new society. As the years passed they created new lives for themselves. Some, content with the role they had evolved into, allowed the old allegiance to slip away. Most of them were intelligent men who were successful at whatever ventures they undertook. They married, raised families and forgot the old days and the old dreams.

But others kept the faith. To all appearances they, too, had found their new lives acceptable. But behind the facade the Nazi beliefs still survived, still dominated their thoughts and guided their actions. These were the keepers of the eternal flame. The bright-eyed elite of the Nuremberg rallies. Hitler's Aryan wunderkinder. Secretly—always believing that one day the Nazi Reich would come to pass—they kept alive the ideal given to them by Adolf Hitler, the Austrian-born creator of the Nazi party. It was he who held them spellbound with his vision of a blond-haired, blue-eyed race of perfect Nordic supermen and women who would rule the world.

The contradiction was that Hitler himself was neither blond nor blue-eyed. He was far removed from the idealized conception of the individuals he hoped would rule. Hitler, the man, was less than impressive in stature and looks, yet he held a nation in the palm of his hand with his magnetic oratory, plunging his willing fellow countrymen into a war of destruction and slaughter that encompassed the globe.

As far as Joachim Mohn was concerned, he would have followed Hitler to the depths of hell. He believed every word the Nazi boss uttered, saw him as the only true leader Germany could ever have. Mohn had been fully convinced of that after the Munich beer hall putsch in 1923. *Mein Kampf* became Mohn's bible and he slavishly dedicated his life to the cause.

Physically Joachim Mohn was the archetypal Aryan. Of pure German stock, the blond young man was an ideal candidate for Hitler's emerging *Schutzstaffel*—the protection squad—which was to become universally known and feared as the SS. Mohn moved swiftly through the ranks and by 1933 had attained the rank of *Untersturmfuhrer*. His unswerving loyalty caught the eye of Hitler's Bavarian cohort, Josef *Sepp*

Dietrich. Dietrich was forming a section of the SS to be known as the SS Bodyguard Regiment Adolf Hitler. This elite group, the *Liebstandarte*, was to take an oath of loyalty and obedience until death—not to the Reich but to Adolf Hitler personally.

Joachim Mohn went from strength to strength, providing his masters with a classic example of Teutonic thoroughness and fighting courage. At war's end Mohn, a major who held the order of the Knight's Cross, discarded his beloved SS uniform and donned the guise of a civilian. He made his way to a seaport, bought passage on a Liberian cargo ship and eventually set foot on Brazilian soil.

Using his not insubstantial hoard of cash, he soon established himself in business, first in exports of coffee and timber, later in gold mining. With German thoroughness he built an empire, his wealth increasing with every year that passed. He also cultivated friends and contacts in high places, using a blend of persuasive charm and even more persuasive bribery.

In Brazil, Mohn met and married a beautiful blond German woman named Anna Kauffman, a former showgirl. A year later their one and only child was born—a boy they named Kurt.

Joachim Mohn's fanatical belief in the Nazi ideal had never faded, from the moment he left Germany. Through his connection with the ODESSA network he was able to keep in touch with others who felt the same. Mohn did more, however, than just talk and dream. He encouraged and financed Nazi groups in many countries, organizing where he could, and always advising.

All these activities provided an education for young Kurt Mohn. Through his teenage years he absorbed Nazi history, his heroes the shadowy figures of Hitler's Reich. Kurt began to follow his father's path, created by and living for his father's vision.

Fired by that vision—of a new Reich emerging from the chaos of a troubled world—Kurt embarked on a low-profile program intended to link together Nazi parties and organizations in as many countries as possible. The way was not always smooth, and Mohn spent time in prison when he fell afoul of anti-Nazi authorities. But his enthusiasms never faltered, and as soon as he was released he would take up where he had been forced to leave off. He recruited many devoted followers, inspiring them with the vision of what he called the New Order. They accepted his plan, pledging their allegiance to his cause. The vision became a reality when Mohn established the New Order's complex deep in the Amazon rain forest. Financed by the huge Mohn fortune and by secret donations, Kurt Mohn established his base and put down the roots of his Nazi empire to be.

He recruited Nazis to train as combat soldiers, to defend and keep secure the secret base. He found specialists in all kinds of warfare, subversion and sabotage, and pilots to fly his squad of helicopters. He brought in scientists to work on biological weapons, because he believed this form of warfare was extremely effective both physically and mentally. In order to keep large amounts of cash flowing in, he involved a section of his group in establishing a cocaine ring. They produced, refined and distributed the drug to buyers in the United States, quickly earning a reputation for quality merchandise at a fair price. The drug sales proved a steady source of income, as well as a means of undermining the decadent and weak American population.

Taking the lead from his father, Kurt sought out and bought some top-level members of the Brazilian government. These contacts were able to oil wheels and also run interference for the Mohn organization. Official "assistance" smoothed the way for Mohn's complex interests and also provided him with eyes and ears in high places.

Mohn's master plan evolved slowly, but with predetermined clarity. Dates fell into place. Locations were chosen. The right palms were greased. In selected worldwide areas, agents of the New Order began to prepare for the day Mohn had code-named the Second Coming.

And then one of Mohn's informants had passed along the message that there was a security breach. A government agent had somehow got wind that there was more to Mohn's operations than a simple drug ring. Although the agent had tried to take the matter further, Mohn's government contacts had blocked the investigation. Aware that he was alone and not knowing whom to trust, the agent had gone directly to the president of Brazil. Then Jorgio Cavantes, one of Mohn's loyal informers—who was playing double agent—advised the Nazi leader that the agent, an undercover policeman named Farrango, had been assigned to help a covert squad of American commandos locate Mohn's base. The Americans were in the country at the request of the Brazilian president.

Mohn had decided to bait the hook and reel the Americans in. So a trap was laid. The bait was Cavantes, who would lead the Americans into the jungle and walk them into the waiting guns of Mohn's own strike force.

Mohn's thoughts of his father and of the evolution of his own involvement in Naziism had so preoccupied him that he had lost all sense of the passing of time. So it was with surprise that he suddenly became aware the helicopter had not only come into sight but was about to land. He watched the Hind settle on the landing pad.

Soon he would be face-to-face with the American scum who had dared to stand up against his elite fighting force.

10

"Damn this bloody awful country," McCarter grumbled.

It was raining again, heavily this time. Even the high canopy of treetops failed to hold it back. The rain hissed down through the greenery, turning the forest floor into a soggy carpet that sank beneath their boots, making difficult even the simple exercise of walking.

"We'll make it," Encizo said encouragingly. But he could appreciate how McCarter was feeling, for he was pretty uncomfortable himself, soaked to the skin, his body stiff and aching. The straps of his backpack bit into the flesh of his shoulders. He was hungry, too, and would have traded a year of his life for a hot meal and a mug of steaming coffee.

McCarter stopped in his tracks, face raised skyward, though it was hard even to see sky through the canopy above them.

"You hear something?" Encizo asked.

McCarter's shrug was noncommittal. After a few more seconds he glanced at Encizo, smiling almost sheepishly. "I *thought* I heard something," he said.

Rainwater was streaming down his face. "Sorry, Rafael."

"So what's there to apologize for? I keep hearing things myself. Like the sound of steak frying in a pan."

McCarter grinned. "Trust you to think about your stomach. Must admit, though, I could tackle a big juicy steak myself."

"And a can of Coke?"

"And a couple of cans of Coke," McCarter said.

Encizo glanced at his wristwatch. "It'll be dark in about an hour," he said. "If Jack doesn't find us soon we could be wandering around this jungle all night."

McCarter took his signal device from his pocket. The indicator light still glowed red to show that the gadget was working.

"Can't be easy for him locating us in this weather, even with a tracking device."

"If we can be found Jack will do it."

They moved on, following as closely as possible but in reverse the route they had taken before the attack force struck. The small compass Encizo carried assisted them in going in the right direction. The Phoenix pair had been walking for almost four hours, determined not to simply stay put until Dragon Slayer swooped in to pick them up. Their minds were set on one thing only—finding Jorgio Cavantes and extracting from him the whereabouts of Kurt Mohn's jungle base. Pushing them was the knowledge that they were working against time. Katz, Manning and James were in the hands of the enemy, and there was no knowing what the Nazi fanatics might do to them. And now that Cavantes had proved himself to be a traitor, Louis Farrango was also in danger.

Cavantes had disappeared at the moment of the ambush and had not been seen again. It was a fair assumption that he had headed back to the river settlement where Farrango, unaware of what had happened, was waiting. If Cavantes did return to the settlement it would most probably be to throw Farrango to the wolves. Cavantes's familiarity with the terrain would allow him a faster return than McCarter and Encizo could manage—unless Jack Grimaldi and his electronic bag of tricks could pick them out of the rain forest.

The rain lasted far longer than any of the previous rainfalls had done, turning into a storm that lashed down out of a slate-gray sky. McCarter and Encizo struggled on through the downpour, stumbling and cursing as they sloshed knee-deep in pools and streams. They slogged through gluey mud, with the added weight of their sodden clothing holding them back. They were cold and wet and exhausted, but neither of them even contemplated quitting.

Not while their Phoenix buddies were in danger. Or while Louis Farrango's life was under threat.

They tramped on, a pair of drenched, mud-streaked scarecrows, fighting the Amazonian elements with a fury that matched the rainstorm itself.

As the darkness closed around them, they cursed the night and carried on, aided by the small flashlights from their backpacks and the compass Encizo still consulted. They lurched from tree to tree in the blackness, bodies scratched by the hostile undergrowth, bruised and tired.

Time ceased to mean anything. There were no minutes, no hours, just an unrelenting period of physical exertion that rolled on and on. . . .

Neither of them heard the thwack of rotor blades until Dragon Slayer was hovering directly overhead. The wash from the helicopter was lost in the driving rain. It was only when Grimaldi flicked on a powerful spotlight, recessed in Dragon Slayer's underbelly, that McCarter and Encizo became aware of the chopper's presence. It was almost midnight.

They stared up into the brilliant beam of light, held like moths before a flame, and watched as Grimaldi brought the helicopter down to settle beside them in the clearing he had tracked them to.

Cutting the machine's power, Grimaldi broke the seal of the cabin's pressurized door and leaned out. "You guys going to stand there all night like a couple of deadbeats, or are you getting inside?"

He thumbed a switch, opening an access door behind his cabin. McCarter and Encizo scrambled inside. The door hissed shut behind them as they tumbled onto the passenger seats in the main compartment. The closed door shut out the hiss of the rain and the dark night.

Grimaldi worked the control that swiveled his seat around so he could see his passengers. "You want to tell me about it?" he asked, reaching for a large thermos bottle of hot coffee.

11

Katz felt the slight bump as the Hind touched down. The rotors began to slow as the power was cut. He remained still in his seat, wishing they would remove the enveloping hood so he could at least see where they were. Not that it would help any. There was no way he could work out their location. The flight had lasted about two hours, as far as he was able to calculate. Not that the time really indicated how far they had come. For all he knew they had flown in a circle, and were no more than few miles from their lift-off point.

The main worry on his mind was that Grimaldi would not be able to track them. The signal devices, which had been taken from them when they were searched, had no doubt been either destroyed or at least inactivated. So there would be no Dragon Slayer blasting its way in to rescue them. Unless McCarter and Encizo had survived to summon the helicopter.

Katz was reasonably confident of the survivability of his men; he thought it likely the Phoenix pair were alive. Maybe they were already in the process of contacting Grimaldi. Maybe Dragon Slayer was seeking them out at this very moment. Maybe...

A rough hand dragged the hood from Katz's head and he blinked against the light that poured in through the Hind's open hatch. Armed men clad in camouflage gear surrounded the helicopter. Across from Katz, James and Manning were also being freed from their hoods.

The tall blond man, obviously in charge of the attack force, gestured in Katz's direction.

"Out. All of you. And make it fast."

The Phoenix commandos climbed from the helicopter to find themselves under the guns of at least a dozen men.

"Follow me," the blond man ordered, and led the way across the dusty compound, toward the large, two-story building facing them.

The large, ugly box-like structure had been constructed out of prefabricated concrete. The exterior had been painted in camouflage colors so that it would blend in with the surrounding jungle. The windows were of nonreflective glass.

As they were marched briskly toward the building, Katz scanned as much of the area as possible, taking in the size of the compound that surrounded the building. The perimeter was not fenced, the jungle itself forming a natural barrier around the base. Katz spotted a couple more Hind choppers and half a dozen smaller helicopters, all concealed beneath camouflage nets. He also noted a number of machine-gun emplacements, these also hidden under nets that would make them invisible from the air. A few jeeps were parked near the main building. The whole setup had a military look to it. This was no ten-cent operation, Katz realized. Mohn's base had cost money. It had been well planned and well built, with a view to being permanent.

The Phoenix warriors were taken into the building through a small door that opened onto a bare hallway that had a downward incline. They seemed to be going beneath the building. The hall eventually brought them to a reception area that opened into a semicircle bordered by steel doors with small, barred windows set in them.

Cells.

All three Phoenix pros were pushed roughly into one of the cells. The door banged shut, and they were left alone.

"Well, it sure ain't home, but it's going to have to do," Calvin James said after a cursory look around.

Manning didn't say a word. He sat down on of the benches bolted to the cell wall. The side of his face was still badly swollen from the butt stroke he had taken earlier. He hadn't said so, but it was obvious he was in pain.

Katz examined the cell carefully. Soon he stopped searching and gestured to James. The ex-SEAL joined him. Katz pointed to something and James nodded.

What Katz showed him was a bug—a planted microphone designed to be unobtrusive, yet capable of picking up conversations that could provide much-needed information.

The fact that the cell was bugged didn't stop the Phoenix warriors from talking; it simply limited the range of subjects they discussed.

After an hour or so a four-man armed escort arrived outside the cell. The door was opened and the Phoenix commandos were ordered to step outside. They were marched along yet another bare corridor, which terminated at an elevator door. The door slid open at the touch of a button. The Phoenix three were ushered inside, alone. The door slid shut and the elevator began to ascend.

"Alone at last," James said with a quick smile.

"You want to guess who'll be waiting at the other end?" Manning said.

"Not the Avon lady?" James asked.

Manning shook his head. "Nothing so easy."

The elevator slowed and stopped. The doors opened, confronting Phoenix Force with yet another armed escort of half a dozen men. They were led briskly along a well-lit corridor that had doors on either side. At the far end of the corridor double doors allowed access to a large room fitted out with laboratory equipment.

There were two men in the room. One was Otto Neiman. The other was Kurt Mohn.

"Good to have you join us, gentlemen," Mohn said as the Phoenix warriors were marched into the room.

"We hadn't the heart to refuse the invitation," Gary Manning replied.

"I like a man with a sense of humor," Kurt Mohn said.

"That's plain to see from the way you dress," Calvin James said.

Mohn's expression changed. His eyes grew hard and cold as he stared at James.

"The tolerance of America for you black apes never ceases to amaze me. How a nation with such potential could allow you animals to walk around free is beyond my comprehension."

James shrugged his shoulders casually. "It's the same tolerance that allows assholes like you to run around playing your sick games."

Mohn snapped some words in German. One of the black-uniformed guards turned on his heel and backhanded James in the face. As the black Phoenix commando stepped back, the guard moved with him, hitting him again. Blood streaked James's face. The guard, a heavy, powerfully built man, smirked at the sight of blood. He turned to glance at Mohn, seeking approval, and while his eyes flicked away from James, the Phoenix pro drove his clenched fist deep into the guy's side. The Nazi thug's breath exploded from his body in a rush. He sagged at the knee, struggling to draw air into his lungs. James gave him little time. He grabbed hold of the guy's shirtfront and yanked him forward, then smashed his knee into the unprotected groin. A scream of pain burst from the guard's lips as his testicles were crushed. He slumped to his knees, moaning in agony. James stepped away from the downed man, holding his hands well away from his body. "How's that for a 'black ape'?" he said to Mohn.

"You may live to regret your rash act," Mohn said.

"I never have regrets over doing the right thing," James told him.

"Why have we been brought here?" Katz asked, hoping to ease the situation by changing the subject.

"You were anxious to find out what I have been doing here," Mohn said. "Wasn't that the purpose of your ill-fated mission?"

"Ill-fated?" James scoffed. "Ain't us that got blown away. That was your guys."

Mohn's face darkened at being reminded of the loss sustained by his men. "A minor setback," he said. "The ones who failed did so because they had not taken their training seriously."

"Is being dead serious enough for you?" James asked.

Katz jumped in again, asking Mohn, "Just what is your secret here?"

"You really want to know?" Mohn smiled. "Of course you do. Very well, I will show you. I'm sure you will find it interesting."

Mohn turned to Neiman, the pair of them falling into a deep conversation.

Glancing at James, Katz was rewarded by a quick wink from the lanky black man. He realized that James was up to something. He wasn't quite certain what James was planning, but he knew it would be something unexpected.

"All right, my friends, shall we go?" Mohn said.

The guards moved to escort Phoenix Force from the room. The moment they neared James he reacted violently.

"Stay the hell away from me, you stupid hellhounds!" James yelled. "Touch me and I'll shove those guns up your assholes!"

"Enough!" Mohn snapped. He gestured at two of the guards. "Return this one to his cell. He can be dealt with later."

Two of the guards held their AK-47's on the black commando. James, still playing the badass, mouthed at them and made a general nuisance of himself as he was escorted from the room. Katz caught Gary Manning watching him. The Canadian's mouth held a slight upward curve, and he nodded to the Phoenix commander.

As Katz and Manning were escorted from the room, following Kurt Mohn along the passage, Katz glanced back over his shoulder and was just in time to see James being taken into the elevator that had brought them up from the cell block beneath the building. He had a feeling that whatever it was James had planned, it might very well start in that elevator.

Calvin James had estimated that it took the elevator just under a minute to make its trip. In those sixty seconds he had to make his move, so that when the door opened he was in control, and holding a weapon in his hands. If he didn't succeed it wouldn't matter, because most likely he would be dead.

Allowing himself to be pushed into the elevator, James stood reasonably still as his guards followed. One stood watching him while the other thumbed the button to close the door and set the car in motion.

The guard operating the elevator had his back to James as the door slid shut. After several more seconds the elevator jerked, then began its slow descent.

The instant the elevator moved, James exploded into action. His right elbow smashed back and up, catching the guard beside him under the chin. The force of the blow destroyed the guard's throat and the Nazi staggered back, slamming up against the rear of the elevator, choking. He dropped his AK-47 as he clutched at his throat, desperately trying to suck air in through his smashed windpipe.

There was no time to recover from the elbow smash. James spun in toward the second guard. Despite having been turned away from James, this guy moved fast, twisting away from the control buttons, his autorifle slashing in at James's face. The Phoenix pro pulled his head aside at the last second, feeling the rush of air as the stock of the AK-47 whistled by. He hammered a clenched fist into the guard's face, crushing his nose to a bloody pulp. The guy grunted and shook his head, spraying blood across the elevator, then lunged for James again. He ran directly into the toe of James's combat boot as it swung up in a powerful roundhouse kick that connected with his upper chest. Ribs splintered under the impact, pain exploding through the guard's body. Not giving the guy a moment to recover, James struck again, a palm-edge chop that broke the guard's collarbone.

The injured Nazi tried to back off, but James stepped in close, grabbing hold of the guy's shirt. He swung the guard off balance, smashing him into the back wall of the elevator. The guard's skull crunched against the tough metal wall, bouncing off to be met by James's fist smashing against his jaw. Bone splintered and teeth were dislodged from bleeding gums by the sheer ferocity of the blow. The guard slithered along the wall and fell facedown on the floor of the elevator.

Breathing hard, James bent over the fallen man. Snatching up the guard's AK-47, James slung it over his shoulder. He found a couple of extra magazines in the guy's combat harness and dropped them in the pocket of his jacket. A swift search of the guard provided James with a slim, razor-sharp knife, which he shoved in his belt.

Turning to the other guard, who was on his back, still and silent now, James took two more ammo mags, then picked up the second AK-47. He checked that it was cocked and ready for use, then positioned himself to one side of the door as the elevator came to rest. The door jerked and slid open.

Silence greeted James. He peered around the doorframe. The hall was empty. Before he stepped out of the elevator James dragged one of the bodies across the opening. If anyone tried to recall the elevator, the door would be unable to close, preventing the car from returning to the upper floor.

Moving quickly, James trotted along the passage until he reached the far end. From memory he remembered which direction led toward the reception area and the door that would take him out of the building.

He was halfway along when a trio of black-uniformed Nazis rounded the far bend.

"Oh, shit," James muttered.

There was no way of avoiding a clash with the Nazis, so James didn't wait to be invited. He swung up the AK-47 he was carrying and opened fire.

His first burst caught the lead Nazi in the chest, spinning him around and bouncing him off the wall. The man left a long bloody smear on the concrete wall as he crashed to the floor, his shattered chest pumping blood down the shredded front of his black shirt.

The other two dragged their AK-47s from their shoulders and started spraying bullets in James's direction. The passage echoed to the rattle of autofire, 7.62 mm slugs whacking chunks out of the concrete.

The moment he had fired on the first Nazi, James hit the floor in a long dive, ignoring the concrete that burned his skin. He twisted his lean body in toward the side of the corridor, then dragged his legs under him and pushed upright. Paying no attention to the slugs bouncing off the concrete, James leveled his Kalashnikov and touched the trigger again. A stream of hot death lashed the black-clad Nazi thugs, tearing into their soft flesh and splintering bones. They were thrown aside by the impact of the 7.62 slugs, bodies twitching in ugly spasms as they went down.

James stepped over them, then rammed in a fresh magazine as he ran, knowing that there was no choice left open to him now. He had to get out of the building—fast. If he was cornered in here he stood no chance. If he managed to break free, there was the possibility he might be able to lose himself in the jungle, where he could maybe contact McCarter and Encizo. He never even considered that they might be dead. As far as James was concerned his Phoenix buddies were out there, and all he had to do was join up with them so they could come back for Katz and

Manning, and then burn this damn place to the ground.

The crash of heavy boots on the concrete told James that time was running out. Mohn's Nazi goons were after him.

The Phoenix pro reached the reception area and saw his way to the exit door blocked off by a half-dozen black-shirted guards. The Nazis opened fire. Bullets howled through the air, thudded against the walls. Like most of their kind the New Order thugs believed that overwhelming firepower was the answer to any combat situation. They simply aimed their weapons in the general direction of the target and pulled the trigger, expending a great deal of ammunition to little effect.

James had been schooled under a different system. His had taught him to make every shot count. That meant taking a second or two longer to aim than your opponent.

That was what James did in response to the Nazi volley. His AK-47 found solid target acquisitions before he touched the trigger. When he fired, his first rounds took out two of the guards, catching one full in the face and reducing his features to a red ruin. The second goon felt something smash against his lower jaw. He tried to yell, but found that he had no mouth left to open. The volley of 7.62s had blown away the lower half of his face, exposing the bone and muscle beneath the flesh.

Seeing two of their companions taken out of the game so swiftly caused the other Nazi thugs to hesitate, though only for a second. That second was all Calvin James needed. The ex-cop ran forward, firing on the move, and though it was not recommended practice, James had made an art out of doing the unexpected. His howling slugs ripped through yielding flesh and brittle bone. They shredded vital organs and blew gory exit holes in writhing bodies. The men, who had been trained by Kurt Mohn to attain the glory of the New Reich, found their salvation in the shape of a 7.62 mm round from an AK-47. They died not even knowing why they were dying, or for what purpose, and their blood ran freely across the floor of Mohn's monument to the Hitler regime.

As the last man went down James ran by, heading for the passage that would take him to the exit door.

He reached it unchallenged, sighing with relief when the door burst open at his kick. He stepped outside to find rain pouring from a rapidly darkening sky. That would at least give him some cover. He glanced around, eyes searching for and finding the jeeps he had seen parked nearby when they had been brought in. He broke away from the side of the building and ran across the rain-soaked compound.

The shrill howl of a siren split the air. His escape had been well and truly advertised now.

The jeeps loomed out of the rain mist. James hopped behind the wheel of the first one. He switched on the ignition, then thumbed the starter button. The vehicle burst instantly into life. James knocked it into gear, flicked off the handbrake and spun the jeep around in a half circle. He jammed his foot down hard on the gas, hurling the jeep across the compound, in the direction of the encroaching jungle.

Autofire shredded the air. Bullets clanged off the jeep's metal body, but none did any lasting damage. One slug went through the windshield, blowing broken glass out over the jeep's hood.

James aimed the vehicle in a straight line, his foot to the floor. The engine howled, tires slipping on the rain-slick ground.

Two figures ran out from behind a parked truck, guns blazing. Hot slugs whipped by James's face. One clipped his left cheek and he gasped at the sudden hot flash of pain, felt blood stream down his face.

James grabbed the AK-47. He laid it across the bottom frame of the shattered windshield, angling it in toward the running figures, who were still blasting shots in his direction. As the jeep drew closer to the foolhardy thugs, James touched the trigger and emptied the remaining 7.62s into the trigger-happy pair. They were mown down by the scything blast, bodies bursting open to spill blood and guts across the wet earth.

James hit the brake as the jeep closed on the tree line. About to exit from the vehicle, he spotted a radio communicator clipped to the jeep's instrument panel. James grabbed the set, hoping that its power pack was fully charged. He jumped clear and ran on, into the welcome shadows of the dense forest.

Tossing aside his empty AK-47, James took the second autorifle from his shoulder, slamming back the cocking bolt. He had a full magazine in the Kalashnikov and two spare. Not as much ammunition as he would have liked, but better than no ammunition at all.

The roar of other jeep engines filled the air. They were closer then he had realized. "Hang in there, guys," he breathed, thinking of Katz and Manning, "'cause I'll be back."

Then he thrust his way into the tangled undergrowth and was soon lost from sight, the noise of his passing masked by the steady hiss of the falling rain.

13

Jack Grimaldi shut down Dragon Slayer's power. As the low throb of the engine died away, the Phoenix pilot swiveled his seat and watched McCarter and Encizo making their final equipment check before confronting Cavantes in his own vice-ridden backyard—and coming to Farrango's aid.

The Brit was carrying his favorite Ingram MAC-10, which he had stripped down and thoroughly cleaned during the flight in. In a shoulder rig was his 9 mm Browning Hi-Power, and his new Gerber Predator was sheathed at his side. Similarly cleaned and checked were Encizo's 9 mm S&W handgun and his MP-5 SMG. Both Phoenix warriors carried extra magazines for their weapons in their combat harnesses, plus concussion and frag grenades.

"You guys need any help in there?" Grimaldi asked.

"We'll handle it, Jack," McCarter said. He knew Grimaldi would like to be with them in the thick of the action. He tapped the radio communicator clipped to his belt. "What we do need is you to jump in if we yell

Dragon Slayer might be the backup muscle we want if things get too hard.''

Grimaldi nodded. "I'll be there if you need me."

Encizo tapped the flier on the shoulder. "We know that, buddy," he said. He meant it.

"Hell, Jack, you've always come through for us," McCarter agreed. "It won't be any different this time."

At last he and Encizo were ready. They slipped out of the helicopter and merged with the foliage. The steamy heat wrapped itself around them like a huge blanket soaked in warm water.

"Any other time I'd say let's wait and make a night assault," Encizo said. "But we don't have the time to spare."

"I don't give a damn what time of day it is," McCarter growled angrily. "Let's hit the bloody place and haul that bastard Cavantes out by his balls."

"Hey, hombre," Encizo said with a grin. "Don't forget we want him to tell us where they've taken our guys!"

The pair pushed on toward the river settlement, conscious all the time of the urgency surrounding their mission.

Katz, Manning and James were in the hands of the enemy. There was no way of knowing their present condition—whether they were alive or dead, whether they were being tortured. All McCarter and Encizo could do was to try to find out the location of Mohn's secret base and then carry out a rescue mission. The fate of their Phoenix Force friends lay in their hands. Whatever the final outcome, McCarter and Encizo would do everything humanly possible to reach their captive partners.

Secondary to the rescue of Katz and company, but important nevertheless, was ensuring the safety of Louis Farrango. The Brazilian undercover cop had deliberately ventured into the enemy camp as part of his role, despite the shadow of suspicion concerning Jorgio Cavantes. Now that the informer had revealed his true colors by betraying Phoenix Force, Farrango was in even greater danger. Cavantes knew the cop's real identity, and if he had no compunction at throwing the five Phoenix commandos to the wolves, he would have even less concern over the life of one undercover policeman.

In just under thirty minutes the Phoenix warriors reached the edge of the settlement on the river. It was just as Farrango had described it. Scattered haphazardly across the wide compound around the large, main adobe-and-wood building were up to a dozen smaller huts and storage sheds. Several cars and trucks were parked in the compound; these included three current-model sedans, as well as some wrecked vehicles in various stages of disrepair. Fifty yards from the main building the dark waters of the Rio Negro lapped at the rickety dock that protruded some fifteen feet from the bank. A few small craft were tied up along the dock, while at the extreme end a twenty-five-foot riverboat was moored, the kind used to carry local cargo up and down the river. The whole compound was littered with rubbish. A few chickens wandered around, sharing an uneasy truce with half a dozen hungry-looking dogs.

"Real choice neighborhood," McCarter muttered.

"Yeah," Encizo agreed. "I'll bet the property values are high."

"So let's bring 'em down, chum."

They were about to move when Encizo touched McCarter's arm. "You notice a couple of things?" the Cuban asked.

"Such as?"

"Nobody around. Where is everybody?"

"Day off?" McCarter suggested.

Encizo chose to ignore the comment. "And who owns those new cars?" he asked pointedly. "None of the lowlifes around here."

McCarter shrugged, but before he could make any further remarks a sudden scream came from the direction of the main building. The sound burst out across the deserted compound, rising to a high pitch before dissolving into a ragged, trembling sob.

"Jesus!" Encizo breathed. He threw a glance in McCarter's direction, and saw the same expression his own face held—mingled compassion and rage.

"That could be Louis in there," McCarter fumed. "If he's been hurt . . ."

"Whoever it is, they need help," Encizo said.

"So let's bloody well do it!" McCarter snapped. "Now! You take the rear. I'm going in by the front door." Without further delay the Briton broke cover and raced across the compound in the direction of the main building.

Encizo gave an exasperated sigh as he watched the cockney tough guy approach the building. *"Loco hombre!"* the Cuban murmured. But he knew that a degree of craziness was sometimes needed for the jobs Phoenix Force was required to do. McCarter probably wasn't any crazier than the rest of them—he just let it show more. Encizo pounded in McCarter's wake, keen eyes watching for any opposition.

McCarter hit the veranda of the building and headed straight for the closed double doors that marked the entrance. He hit the doors on the run, bursting them open as he barreled through.

The interior centered around one large, low-ceilinged room, originally a trading post cum saloon. Along the back wall ran a mahogany-topped bar, and behind it was shelving that had once held bottles. A large mirror was fixed to the wall between the shelves, the glass now cracked and filthy. Round tables and wooden chairs were scattered around the main floor area. At the far side of the room was a ten-foot-square raised platform on which stood a dilapidated piano. At both ends of the bar, doors gave access to the rear of the building, where there were smaller rooms and stairs that led to the upper floor.

As McCarter barged into the room he absorbed the layout first and the occupants next. There were about a dozen men in the place, the majority of them gathered around a figure suspended from ropes slung over one of the main roof beams. The ropes were tied around the man's wrists, raising him so that his feet were clear of the floor. The ropes had been tied so tightly that they had cut into the man's flesh and stopped the circulation.

The dangling figure was naked, his body streaked heavily with blood. His flesh had been cut and ripped and burned. A pool of congealing blood spread across the floorboards below his feet. Great dark bruises showed where he had been savagely beaten. The man's face was swollen and discolored, his left eye a gouged, gory crater. He was close to being unrecognizable.

McCarter recognized him. He was Louis Farrango.

Even as McCarter took in the scene of horror, Farrango's body arched in agony. McCarter then saw the figure behind the undercover cop, hunched over as he thrust some gleaming metal object between Farrango's buttocks. The tortured cop gave a hoarse cry of pain, his body twisted as he tried to pull away from the instrument invading his flesh.

A flood of rage exploded within McCarter, an overwhelming rage directed toward those who were torturing Farrango and enjoying the spectacle of his suffering.

Meanwhile the sound of the splintering doors had alerted them to McCarter's arrival on the scene. Heads turned. Eyes took in the Briton's armed and plainly offensive posture. Someone yelled. All began to reach for weapons. They were too late.

McCarter's MAC-10 tracked in on the figure behind Farrango. Found and held him. The torturer raised his head the second before McCarter triggered the Ingram.

A stream of 9 mm sizzlers homed in on the target, impacting against his face. They burned in through flesh, muscle and bone, exploding the skull in a grisly spray. The torturer's body was flung backward, arms spread as he toppled to the floor and lay kicking in his own voided waste.

Hastily drawn guns were aimed at McCarter as he turned the hot muzzle of the MAC-10 toward new targets. The crowd was scattering, yelling, directing their rage as well as their weapons at the Phoenix invader. The supercommando held his ground, triggering the Ingram and hosing the degenerates who could stand and watch a man being brutally tortured as if it was entertainment.

His first burst ripped the guts out of a wild-eyed guy waving a big Colt .45 automatic pistol. As the 9 mm slugs burned through the man's large belly he let out a shrill scream. His finger jerked the trigger of the .45, sending a slug zipping past McCarter's face. The British commando put a further trio of slugs into the screaming man, blowing off the top of his skull. The guy collapsed on the floor in a steaming pile of his own intestines.

By then several guns had opened up, bullets burning the air around McCarter's weaving figure. Some of the projectiles came close, but not close enough to stop the rampaging cockney. He blasted his way through the room, the Ingram chattering loudly. Two of the thugs came hurtling in his direction. One was working the lever of a battered Marlin repeating rifle, while the other, screaming incoherently, slashed the air with a machete. McCarter dropped to one knee, avoiding the blade of the machete, which passed harmlessly above his head. McCarter's response was to shove the muzzle of the Ingram into the axman's crotch and pull the trigger. The 9 mm slugs chewed the enemy's vital organ into little pieces before coring up into his body and ripping through the base of his spine, blowing a ragged hole in his lower back as they emerged. The machete slipped from twitching fingers as he forgot about McCarter and descended into his own private hell of pain. Even as the guy was falling away from him, McCarter turned the MAC-10 on the second attacker, then cursed as the Ingram clicked empty. Coolly the British ace reached down and pulled his Hi-Power, lifting it in time to pump three shots into the Marlin owner's face. That opponent's features vanished in a wash of blood and a mess of bone splinters and mashed flesh.

Still on one knee, McCarter fired off individual shots at the moving targets, missing only once. It was typical of the hotheaded Briton that, placed in a difficult combat situation, his natural skills took command. He aimed and fired, aimed and fired, as if he was on a firing range, shooting at paper targets. The fact that these targets were shooting back did nothing to upset the Phoenix pro's deliberate and precise attack.

The panicked lowlife were not used to such confrontations. They were back-street killers, courageous only when the odds were in their favor. They would kill or maim if there was no risk to themselves. They could be brave and manly and watch a man being hung up like a piece of meat and tortured, because there was no danger to themselves. Faced with a true warrior of McCarter's stature, they lost all control.

Those McCarter didn't hit directly loosed off ill-aimed shots that hit everything but the intended target. In their desperation they emptied their weapons, then fled. They smashed windows and scrambled through. A few made it. Some, congratulating themselves on escape, were blown through the windows by one of McCarter's well-placed shots. Their bloodied bodies crashed to the veranda outside the building. Others burst through the doors leading into the rear of the building, only to run into the vengeful gun of Rafael Encizo.

When Encizo had rounded the main building, sprinting for the rear entrance, the first thing he saw was the blue-and-white Bell helicopter standing on open ground about twenty feet from the building. He added this to the sleek, modern cars parked alongside the wrecks out front, and asked himself the question: who else was involved in this affair? He had no time to seek an answer at that moment, for the sound of gunfire coming from inside the building told him that McCarter had started to clean house. The Cuban took himself to the rear of the building, and almost ran into the opposition.

A bunch of armed men, dressed in lightweight suits and all wearing dark glasses, came rushing into view. The moment they saw Encizo they opened fire.

A hail of bullets whacked the ground at Encizo's feet. Geysers of dirt flew in the air. He immediately changed course, slamming up against the side of the building. He swept up his H&K MP-5 and returned fire. Encizo's 9 mm bullets did more than kick up dirt; they burned flesh and spilled blood. He let go with a sustained blast that tore the gunmen apart. The neat suits became bloody tattered fabric, and fragments of flesh misted the air as the gunmen were tossed off their feet, bodies squirming and twitching. Only one of the gunmen remained on his feet, spitting gouts of blood from his mouth as he tried to track his SMG on Encizo. The Cuban warrior put the final half-dozen 9 mm shredders into the guy, ripping his throat out in a burst of red gore. Ejecting the empty magazine, Encizo banged in a fresh one, and cocked the MP-5 as he ran for the rear door. As he entered what had once been a kitchen but now resembled a trash can, Encizo heard sustained gunfire farther inside the building. He headed in the direction of the sound.

Almost at once, armed figures burst into view. They saw Encizo and started shooting without hesitation. Bullets ripped splinters from the walls, blew out chunks of plaster. In the confines of the building the gunshots were deafening.

Encizo hosed the passage ahead of him, his bullets taking out a trio of wild-eyed thugs. They were spun around by the H&K's powerful blast, bodies sprouting holes that erupted blood. It spattered the walls and ran down them in red streaks. Stepping over the still-jerking bodies, Encizo pushed open a door and entered the main room, just in time to see McCarter rise to his feet and put a single bullet from his Browning through the head of a guy toting an AK-47.

As the Hi-Power's slug ripped his head apart, the dying enemy's finger clamped down on the trigger of the AK-47. A stream of slugs cut through the air. One clipped McCarter's left side, just above his belt. The Brit gave a yell, more of anger than of pain. "Bastard!"

Then silence fell, broken only by the moans of the wounded, and of Louis Farrango.

"Jesus!" Encizo cried as he recognized the undercover cop.

McCarter was already at Farrango's side. He put down his gun and drew his knife. Encizo supported Farrango as McCarter cut the ropes, then lowered the tortured man gently to the floor. Encizo found some heavy tablecloths behind the bar and draped several across Farrango's bloody body for warmth.

Despite the obvious pain he was in, the Brazilian cop recognized the Phoenix commandos. He managed to speak, in a hoarse voice. "He said you were all dead."

"Cavantes?" Encizo asked.

Farrango nodded.

"The little shit tried to arrange that," McCarter said. "He led us into an ambush. Mohn's men were waiting for us."

"You are all alive?" Farrango asked.

"The others were captured and taken off in one of Mohn's choppers."

"Then you need Cavantes," Farrango rasped. "He is still the only one who can lead you to Mohn's base."

"Is he here?" Encizo asked.

Farrango nodded weakly. "They picked him up in the jungle and brought him in by helicopter."

"He had it all worked out," McCarter said bitterly.

"What about the guys in suits? The helicopter?" Encizo asked. "Where did they come from?"

"They are from the capital. Secret police directed by a man named Ludwig Kessler. Internal security. Dirty-jobs department. I think Kessler is Mohn's man. He has high-up connections with certain members of government. Men who could easily have sympathy for Kurt Mohn and his group." Farrango paused as pain washed over him. "I should have connected Kessler with Mohn before."

"Why the torture, Louis?" McCarter asked.

"They wanted to know all about you—where you were from, why you were here, who authorized your coming. They were frightened they might be exposed."

McCarter addressed Encizo. "Look after Louis."

"Where are you going?"

"We need Cavantes," the Brit answered. "I'm going to find him."

"Be careful," Farrango warned him. "He has a bodyguard with him."

"Yeah? Well, he's going to need one," McCarter replied, snatching up his Ingram and heading for the door.

As soon as McCarter stepped outside he saw Jorgio Cavantes. The treacherous double agent was in the act of climbing into the passenger seat of one of the new cars parked outside the building. In the driver's seat was a powerful-looking man in a tan suit. The moment Cavantes recognized McCarter his face turned pale. He said something to the driver and slammed his door shut. The car, a metallic-blue Chrysler, lurched forward, kicking up plumes of dust as it tore away from the settlement and vanished along the dirt track.

McCarter ran to one of the other cars. It, too, was a Chrysler, in metallic-gray. The keys were in the ignition.

McCarter tossed his MAC-10 on the seat, unclipped the communicator from his belt and thumbed the transmit button. "Phoenix to Dragon Slayer. Come in Dragon Slayer. Over."

Grimaldi responded instantly. "Dragon Slayer to Phoenix. I hear you. Go ahead. Over."

McCarter's impatience overrode his professionalism for the moment, and he ignored procedure. "Get in here fast. There's a blue Chrysler heading away from the settlement along the dirt track. Cavantes is making a run for it and we need him alive. I'm going after him in a gray Chrysler, so if you have to shoot anything, make sure it isn't painted gray. You read me, flyboy?"

"Hell, yes," Grimaldi answered. "I'm on my way, Phoenix. Over and out."

McCarter scrambled into the Chrysler and started the engine. He pushed the lever to Drive, released the brake and floored the gas pedal. The big car rocked on its suspension as it roared across the bumpy ground and out along the dirt track.

"Okay, Cavantes, you creep," McCarter said. "Look over your shoulder and see who's coming to get you!"

14

As McCarter pushed the Chrysler along the dirt track he fastened his seat belt. It was a wise move. The rough surface of the primitive road threw the big American-built sedan around like a cardboard box floating down a flooded stream. It took all McCarter's expertise to keep the vehicle from plunging off the track into the tangled undergrowth on either side.

He couldn't see the car Cavantes was in. It was lost in the boiling cloud of dust that blew up from its rear wheels. The dust added another risk for McCarter. It was like driving in a fine brown mist. Nevertheless, the daredevil Briton kept his foot hard down on the gas pedal, risking everything in his attempt to catch the fleeing traitor.

As he drove, McCarter made an attempt to hold back the rage churning his insides, but the image of Louis Farrango, naked, bleeding and in agony, refused to be banished from his mind. Each time that picture formed, McCarter's anger blossomed afresh. He knew he was allowing his feelings to get the better of him, but he was unable to resist. David McCarter was no novice to the world of violence. He knew only too well the obscenities man was able to inflict on his fellow humans. All through his adult life he had moved in that twilight world where violence, death, torture and a thousand unspeakable horrors were commonplace, where suffering and pain were daily fare. McCarter understood that. For the most part he was able to live with that knowledge.

But something nagged at him this time. He was unable to pinpoint the reason, but Louis Farrango's suffering had hit McCarter hard and had left a mark on him. It had settled around his shoulders like a ghastly shroud, and he could not shake it off.

Maybe he was getting too old, he thought. Maybe he had seen too many good people suffer—men like Farrango, who had devoted their lives to combating evil, forgoing a life of comfort and safety because they believed passionately in justice and order in a world that seemed bent on self-mutilation. How many had died? he wondered. How many had suffered untold agonies in that endless battle against the savages?

Just then the Chrysler's front wheels hit a deep rut. The powerful car lurched to the left, the wheels on that side dropping over the edge of the track. Thick undergrowth was ripped and shredded as the heavy vehicle plowed through it. McCarter, cursing loudly, fought the shuddering wheel, his strong hands holding the car on as straight a course as he could. He took his foot from the gas pedal, letting the speed drop a little, then yanked on the wheel. As the car's front tire rolled up onto the main track again McCarter pumped the gas. The Chrysler leaped forward, bouncing back to the center of the track.

"That'll teach you, David, my lad," McCarter chided. "Getting all depressed. Get your mind on the job."

Now he could hear the steady thwack of Dragon Slayer's rotors. The combat chopper's dark bulk flashed into view, passed over McCarter's car. The downdraft from the helicopter drove away the cloud of dust obscuring Cavantes's getaway vehicle.

Grimaldi's voice crackled from the communicator on the seat beside McCarter. "Dragon Slayer to Phoenix, Back off a way, Phoenix. Give me room. I don't want to scorch your paint job. Over and out."

McCarter took his foot off the pedal and allowed his vehicle to slow, while he watched Dragon Slayer sink toward the ground, holding steady behind the blue Chrysler. Grimaldi opened up with the multibarrel cannon in the nose. A hail of 7.62 mm ammo lashed the track just ahead of the car carrying Cavantes. Grimaldi let Dragon Slayer fall behind a few yards, then opened up again, planting more slugs in the track on either side of the weaving car.

The driver lost control of the Chrysler. It swept in toward the side of the track, bouncing as it struck deep ruts, then slid back to the center again.

Dragon Slayer let fly with another storm of 7.62s. The bullets marched alongside the car, kicking up a hail of dirt that rattled against the vehicle.

The Chrysler shot forward, gaining speed, then just as abruptly fishtailed and went smashing into the dense undergrowth at the side of the rutted track. It crashed its way through the foliage, coming to a sudden dead stop.

Jamming his foot hard on the brake, McCarter brought his vehicle to a shuddering halt. He grabbed his Ingram and was out of the car before it had stopped moving, swiftly cutting across the track, peering through the drifting haze of dust that rose around the other car.

The driver's door was smashed open, swinging back on its hinges. The hulking bodyguard exited the vehicle, moving with surprising speed for such a big man. As his feet touched the ground his body twisted around in McCarter's direction. He had a 9 mm Uzi in his hands, and he opened up with it the moment he laid eyes on the British commando.

McCarter dived for the ground the second he saw the Uzi. As he rolled he heard the angry chatter of the SMG, felt the whiplash of the slugs as they burned the air above his body. The British pro rose to a crouch, circling around the car. He caught a glimpse of Cavantes through the window of the Chrysler. The informer was trying to open his car door but couldn't; the impact of the car when it hit the off-track ground had jammed the door shut.

Movement in the corner of McCarter's eye made him turn. The bodyguard was standing at the rear of the Chrysler, pulling the muzzle of his Uzi around to line it up on McCarter. The Phoenix pro leveled his MAC-10 and pulled the trigger, sweeping the muzzle back and forth across the bodyguard's wide chest. A stream of 9 mm slugs burrowed deep into the guy's body, puncturing both lungs and shredding his heart. The big man screamed in agony, the sound trailing off as a gout of blood erupted from his mouth. He toppled against the trunk of the car, dropping his weapon. Blood spurted from a couple of the holes in his chest, spattering across the dusty paint job. Sliding down the rear of the Chrysler, the dying bodyguard got hooked up with the rear bumper and stayed in a semikneeling position.

McCarter ran to the side of the car and stared through the dusty window at Cavantes. The Brazilian traitor gazed back at him with terror shining in his eyes. Cavantes grabbed for the revolver tucked into his trousers. The Ingram crackled briefly, the bullets shattering the glass of the window. Cavantes was showered with broken glass as the bullets ripped through and buried themselves in the dashboard. McCarter pushed the MAC-10's muzzle through the glassless frame to within an inch of Cavantes's throat.

"Go ahead," he invited. "Take the gun out, Jorgio. Give me an excuse to blow your sodding face right off!"

Cavantes, staring down the threatening muzzle of McCarter's Ingram, decided that caution was the order of the day. He raised his hands, letting McCarter see they were empty.

"Out," McCarter ordered. "Through the other door. And keep those hands where I can see them."

Cavantes began to slide across the seat in the direction of the open driver's door. With the MAC-10 trained on him all the time, McCarter walked around the front of the car to meet the double agent as he stepped out of the Chrysler.

"Get those hands all the way up," McCarter ordered sternly, and as Cavantes obeyed, McCarter reached out with his left hand and removed the gun Cavantes had tucked in his waistband. He threw it far into the dense foliage behind the informer. "You won't be needing that anymore," he said.

Cavantes licked his suddenly dry lips. He had looked into McCarter's eyes, and had realized he would receive no mercy from this man. This one would never forgive him for the jungle ambush, nor for the torture of Louis Farrango. For the first time in his miserable life Jorgio Cavantes knew total, abject fear.

"We have some talking to do, chummy," Mc-Carter said tautly. "And you are neck-deep in the shit if I don't get the answers I want."

"I can't tell you anything," Cavantes blurted out.

McCarter smiled coldly. "We'll see about that, you little asshole." He stared at Cavantes for a while, plainly at odds with thoughts swimming around in his mind. Then he said, "I really don't approve of it, and I'm going to feel guilty as hell tomorrow, but it isn't going to stop me doing it."

"I do not understand," Cavantes said. "Do what?"

"Oh, just this," McCarter said, and punched Cavantes in the mouth. The force of the blow spun Cavantes off his feet. He slammed up against the side of the Chrysler, his fingers grabbing the edge of the roof for support. Blood dribbled freely from his mashed lips and from his gums. The lower part of his face felt numb, and when he tried to move his jaw a blinding pain shot through it.

McCarter felt a little relieved, the tension eased inside him. Grabbing Cavantes's shirt, he hauled the man away from the car and shoved him toward the track, in the direction of Dragon Slayer, which Grimaldi had put down only yards away.

"This him?" Grimaldi asked as he stepped out of Dragon Slayer.

McCarter nodded. "Rat of the year," he said. "This little heap of horse shit led us into an ambush, then came back here and put the finger on Louis."

"What happened to his face?" Grimaldi asked, observing the bloody mess that marked the informer.

"He must have walked into something," McCarter said.

"That's easy to do out here," Grimaldi remarked.

"Let's go," McCarter said. "I want to see how Farrango is. Then as soon as we can we'll head out to find Mohn's fun palace. And this time our chum, Jorgio here, is taking us all the way in."

15

It had been one of the longest nights Calvin James could remember. The rain had persisted for what had seemed an eternity. With his AK-47 strapped tightly to his back, the Phoenix pro had pushed his way deep into the hostile forest, intent on distancing himself from Mohn's pursuing Nazi thugs. He couldn't see them or hear them, but he knew they were behind him somewhere. The only consolation was that they would be as uncomfortable as he was.

He had stumbled and groped his way through the trees and foliage for close to three hours, finally coming to a deep, rocky ravine. The descent to its bottom was slow and painful, but James somehow made it, stitching his way along the muddy bed of the ravine in water that reached his knees. A pale moon had finally shown itself and had thrown just enough light to show the tough guy from Chicago where he was going. James had found a shallow cave some ten feet above the bed of the ravine, dragged himself up the rocky side, and into the dark shadows of the hole.

Despite his eagerness to put more space between himself and the encampment, James reasoned that it was worth the risk to rest up until dawn. Otherwise, he was liable to get hopelessly lost in the darkness, and maybe even killed if he couldn't see where he was going. He also figured that no matter how good Mohn's men were, even a Nazi superman couldn't track him through the Amazon jungle in darkness and pouring rain. The cave was damp and cold, and the hard rock wasn't the most comfortable surface to lie on, but James was in no position to complain. He made the best of it and managed to snatch some sleep.

The distant but unmistakable sound of a helicopter roused him from his slumber. For a fraction of a second he thought it was Dragon Slayer. Then he listened carefully and realized the engine tone was too light for Dragon Slayer.

He eased himself out of his cave and worked his way to the top of the ravine. The rain had ceased sometime during the night, and as the new day flooded the rain forest with light, the Phoenix pro could feel the steamy heat building up again. He took some time to observe the sunrise, pinpointing its location. This enabled him to estimate roughly his position. He turned and began to move south, gauging his line of travel by the movement of the sun across the sky and the fall of the shadows from the trees. His calculations were crude, he admitted to himself, but they were all he had to go on.

The distant sound of the helicopter drifted back and forth, indicating it was being flown in sweep patterns. James was convinced it was one of Mohn's helicopters. They were still out looking for him, using the aerial capabilities of the chopper to locate him. The helicopter was probably in contact with Mohn's men on the ground.

James pushed on. The temperature rose, and he began to sweat. His combat gear clung to him. He began to find his own body odor unpleasant. Toward midmorning he took five, resting beneath a towering liana-wrapped tree. The top of the massive tree was lost in the misty dimness high above his head. While he rested he realized he was hungry. His stomach growled.

Something rustled nearby. James twisted around, the AK-47 probing the air.

The foliage parted and three brown-skinned men with jet-black hair stepped into view. They were dressed in white cotton garments, and they had bare feet.

They had to be local Indians, James decided. The mission had been set up too quickly for any of Phoenix Force to become knowledgeable about the names of the tribes in the area. But these men were certainly not specimens of Mohn's Nazi Aryans. From their appearance, he couldn't tell whether or not they were hostile, but he had a feeling he would soon find out.

He stood up, lowering the muzzle of the AK-47 to the ground, and gave what he hoped was a friendly smile. "Any of you speak English?" he asked.

Three pairs of dark, glittering eyes studied him impassively, faces expressionless. There was nothing in any of those carved features to indicate their feelings.

James thought desperately. What the hell do you say to an Amazon Indian?

Then the Indian in the center spoke, in halting, heavily accented English. "Where you come from?"

"Do you know the place where the Germans hide?" James asked. "I was a prisoner there. I escaped."

The Indian who had spoken made a low, angry sound. He muttered something to his companions. They stared at James as if he was some crazy man.

"You say the Germans your enemy?" the Indian asked.

"Yes."

The Indian nodded. "Then you are my friend."

"No shit?" James grinned. "I'm real glad to hear that."

The Indian came forward, pointing a thumb at the sky. "Helicopter look for you?"

"Yeah, I guess so."

"Blackshirts also in jungle."

James figured the Indian was talking about Mohn's ground troops. "If they catch me they will kill me," he explained. "I have to find some of my friends and take them to the German base. The Germans have other friends of mine as prisoners. I have to get them out of that place."

The Indian pointed back the way James had come. "That is very bad place. A place of death. Many of my tribe have died there. Many are still prisoner."

"What the hell goes on there?" James asked.

"Bad magic," the Indian said. "Blackshirts have spirit of evil that kills."

"It's why my friends and I came here," James explained. "To destroy the blackshirts and to burn that place. But I need to find my friends."

"Where are your friends?"

James grinned. "That's the problem. I don't know. We were separated after the blackshirts attacked us."

"Where did you start from?" the Indian asked.

"Manaus. Then an old settlement on the Rio Negro."

The Indian translated for his companions, and they fell into a lively conversation that lasted for a couple of minutes. James felt like asking them to hurry the hell up, but didn't; he figured these Indians just might be his ticket out of the jungle, and he wasn't about to offend them.

Finally the English-speaking Indian came up to the black Phoenix pro. He grinned widely, revealing sharp, stained teeth. "Show you way," he said.

"That's great, man."

The Indian touched James on the arm. "Can you free my friends?" he asked.

"If I can get back in there, pal, I'll do my best."

It seemed the right thing to say, because the Indian nodded and gripped James's arm tightly.

"Come—follow."

The Indian moved off, James right behind him. The other Indians trotted off into the surrounding forest, vanishing from sight. "They look for blackshirts," James's guide explained.

The Indian set a ground-eating pace. James found it hard to keep up with the wiry native, who plainly knew the jungle as a man knows his backyard. James saw no sign of the other two for almost an hour. Then one of them appeared without warning, speaking to James's guide, who then turned directly to James.

"The blackshirts are near. He has seen them."

"Damn!" James glanced at the Indian guide. "How close?"

The Indian translated to his companion. This one spoke rapidly, gesturing as he spoke.

James didn't really need a full translation. The way the Indian was talking, he could tell that the Nazis weren't far away.

At that moment the sky overhead was filled by the pulsating roar of a helicopter engine. James glanced up and saw the fleeting shape through the canopy of branches. The helicopter turned, then swept back and hovered.

The mothers had him spotted!

The third Indian burst into view, yelling wildly, pointing back into the jungle.

Almost at once the rattle of autofire rang out. Bullets chewed into the exposed back of the Indian who had just shown himself. The unfortunate native was slammed to the ground, fist-size holes in his chest as the bullets exploded from his flesh.

James turned his AK-47 in the direction the shots had come from and triggered off a burst. He heard agitated voices, and fired again. A man screamed.

"We go! We go!" James's guide insisted, tugging at the Phoenix warrior's sleeve.

They ran full tilt through the dense forest, ignoring the snatching foliage that cut their flesh, ripped their clothing. They twisted and turned through thick, tangled undergrowth to avoid smashing into trees. They splashed through water and mud. The helicopter overhead appeared to be staying with them. Its hazy dark shape could be seen through the green canopy of intertwined branches.

Gunshots rang out. Slugs whined through the air, striking trees. James about-turned, expending more ammunition, sweeping the muzzle of the AK-47 from left to right.

"Here!" called the Indian guide.

James half turned and caught a glimpse of a black-uniformed figure stepping into view from behind a tree. The Nazi fanatic, pale eyes blazing with wild light, had his Kalashnikov almost at shoulder height. The weapon got no farther. Calvin James fired the moment he locked eyes with the neo-Nazi thug. His AK-47 ripped the air with its lethal blast, and the blond guy spun away, his chest spouting blood from a half-dozen ragged holes.

"Get the gun," James yelled.

The Indian snatched up the AK-47, fumbled extra magazines from the dead man's belt pouches.

The other Indian shouted a warning, then caught a faceful of 7.62 mm slugs. He stumbled blindly back, hands clutched to his ruined, bloody face. A second burst of fire blew off the back of his skull.

James turned his gun on the attacker just as his Indian guide did the same. They fired together, blasting another Nazi thug into oblivion.

"This is getting too damn hot," James rasped. He clapped his Indian guide on the shoulder. "Let's get the hell out of here." They ducked into the undergrowth, losing themselves in dense jungle, with yells and bullets following them.

Overhead the persistent drone of the tracking helicopter faded.

As the jungle became denser, closing in on them, their progress slowed, but still they continued. James's Indian never faltered once. His feel for the terrain was incredible. He seemed able to read the way ahead, anticipating obstacles and taking them on a route that avoided delays.

It was still hard going through the lush, intertwined vegetation. James pushed and shoved in the wake of the Indian, silently cursing the Amazon basin and its attendant evils. He could feel the sweat running from him like water from a tap, and knew he would never again be able to enjoy stepping into a sauna bath.

Minutes later it began to rain. The heavy drops splattered against the thick vegetation, increased and then sluiced down in a torrent.

The Indian turned and grinned at James, pointing to something the Phoenix pro couldn't spot. Through a narrow defile in the rock, he led James to a stony outcropping. They emerged in an enclosed ravine that held a deep cave at its far end.

"Rest," the Indian said.

As soon as they were seated the Indian thrust his hand into a hide pouch strapped around his waist. He pulled out strips of dried meat, passing some to James. The ex-cop took it and spent the next few minutes chewing the tough-fibered meat. The Indian watched with an amused twinkle in his dark eyes. Despite a feeling that he would regret it, James asked what animal the meat was from.

"Capybara," his companion said.

James lifted his eyebrows questioningly.

The Indian laughed. "Capybara. Capybara," he repeated.

Something edged its way forward from the dark recesses of James's mind. Capybara. He recalled the name from school lessons. Damn, what was it? And then it slowly came to him. The Capybara was... was... the largest rodent—that was it. A large rodent with the appearance of a guinea pig but without as much hair. James swallowed a chunk of the meat. Great! He was eating dried rat meat!

His expression said it all, and the Indian grinned at him even more. James smiled back and held up the half-chewed strip of meat. "Good stuff," he said.

The rain stopped after a half hour. They moved on. When they were back in the jungle the Indian showed James how to quench his thirst with water from the broad, deep leaves of plants that had held the rain.

The hours slid by. The heat increased, sucking the moisture out of the jungle. Vapor rose from the vegetation and floated up among the trees. There, diffused sunlight, breaking through the mist, formed shadows that wavered and swayed, a primeval atmosphere that was totally in keeping with the landscape.

Breaking free from the dense foliage, James and his Indian guide found themselves on the edge of a clearing. A large pool of water spread across part of the clearing. Clouds of insects hovered over the water, darting shapes that flitted in and out of the sunlight. In the center of the pool a fish rose to the surface, splashed and vanished from sight, leaving spreading rings on the water.

"We go other side," the Indian said, pointing across the clearing. "Now follow straight trail to river." He led the way across the clearing, moving at a steady lope.

James followed, conscious of being exposed. He sensed the helicopter before he saw it. Turning on his heel, the Phoenix warrior spotted the chopper as it rose over the treetops, then dropped in toward the clearing. He recognized the craft as a Bell 206B Kiowa.

This one was painted in camouflage colors and had a 7.62 mm minigun fitted on the left side.

Sweeping in across the clearing, the Kiowa dropped to within a couple of feet from the ground. The minigun opened up with a deafening racket, spitting a vicious hail of steel-jackets at the running figures. The line of slugs marched across the earth, kicking up dirt and grass, then it hacked wood splinters from the trunks of trees lining the edge of the clearing. With a howl from its powerful engine, the Kiowa burned over James's head, rising suddenly to clear the timberline. It swept up and around to come in for a second run. James knew they couldn't hope to dodge the chopper forever—especially not with all those 7.62 flesh-shredders flying about. He looked back, then ahead across the clearing. There was little difference in the distances either way. They were caught in the middle.

"Keep going!" he yelled to the Indian.

Coming in almost at ground zero, the Kiowa laced the clearing with more 7.62s.

James felt the ground vibrate to the solid whack of the pounding steel-jackets, and too late saw his Indian guide break to the left—directly into the path of the advancing minigun.

The Indian's death scream was lost in the hammering gunfire and the slam of the Kiowa's rotors. The rapid-fire minigun stitched the Indian's body with more than a dozen slugs, pitching his shattered form across the clearing to settle in a heap of bloody debris.

"Bastards!" James ranted as the Kiowa banked away. He ran to the Indian's body, and knew before looking that his new friend was dead. "Damn! Hell, man, I never even got to ask your name."

James's anger at the death of the Indian fueled his response as he heard the helicopter roaring in again. Jamming his last full magazine into the AK-47, he turned to face the Kiowa, holding his position as it drove in across the clearing. He held, and waited, knowing that if he didn't time this right he was going to end up dead himself.

Call it judgment. Timing. Instinct. Whatever—it worked for Calvin James.

He brought up the Kalashnikov AK-47 and burned the full magazine on autofire. The stream of 7.62s lashed the Kiowa's Plexiglas canopy, shattering it and blowing fragments into the faces of the pilot and the enemy operating the minigun. Plastic and steel-jackets turned flesh and bone into bloody rags and splinters.

With no hand on the controls, the Kiowa spun off course. It dropped, and already being close to the ground, it grazed the earth, tilted and went end over end. Metal disintegrated. Ruptured fuel tanks spilled flammable liquid. This, in turn, hit hot engine parts, and the cartwheeling chopper vanished in a white-hot ball of fire.

The shock wave from the explosion tossed Calvin James six feet across the clearing.

After the initial fireball, a thick cloud of black smoke rose into the blue sky above the jungle. It was visible for miles.

16

Katz and Manning ate their breakfast in the cell where they had spent the night. Aware that their every word was being monitored, the Phoenix pair said little. Their minds, however, were active. The previous night's developments had given them a great deal to think about.

First had been Calvin James's dramatic escape from the base. Katz had started to suspect that the black commando was up to something when James had persisted with his aggressive behavior. James was usually able to control his feelings, so Katz guessed his act in front of Mohn was put on for the benefit of their captors. James's subsequent escape while being escorted back to his cell had only proved what Katz had suspected. The news of James's escape had made Katz feel much more optimistic. At least they had someone on the outside now, a teammate who would do whatever was necessary to contact the rest of the force and effect a rescue.

When Mohn had been told about the escape his eyes had mirrored the rage boiling deep inside. But, to his credit, the Nazi chief had managed to appear calm and objective, on the surface. "I doubt he will get far," the self-styled Nazi said. "He is alone, without food or water, in a hostile environment. Send out a squad in the morning. They know this jungle well. They will find him. Use one of the helicopters for tracking and observing."

When his minion left, Kurt Mohn had returned his attention to Katz and Manning. The Phoenix pair were seated in comfortable leather chairs facing a large black desk, behind which sat the Nazi headman. The large room they were in, Mohn's office, was decorated with Nazi paraphernalia. Behind the desk, and covering most of the wall, was a huge Nazi flag, black overall, with a large white circle in the middle that contained a blood-red swastika.

When Katz had first entered the room and seen the flag, he had almost lost control. It had taken all his willpower to contain the anger that flooded him. The blatant acknowledgment of Nazism recalled all the horror Katz had seen as a youngster when he had worked with the French Resistance. World War II had plunged the world into an age of barbarism, orchestrated by the fanatical thugs of Hitler's Reich. The evil they had perpetrated was something Katz would never completely forget. Even with the defeat of Germany, the Nazi fetish had survived over the decades and had flourished. Phoenix Force had tangled with neo-Nazi groups before. They had always survived to tell the tale.

Four of Mohn's black-clad goons, armed with SMGs, stood behind Katz and Manning. At the side of Mohn's desk sat the tall, thin man named Otto Neiman.

"I must congratulate you on the skill of your companion," Mohn said. "For a black he shows considerable combat ability."

"It takes a hell of a lot more than blond hair and blue eyes to make a combat soldier," Manning said evenly. "More than you and your bunch of clowns will ever be."

"You persist in making reckless statements," Mohn said. "If I lift my finger you are a dead man. Consider your position."

Manning shrugged. "In my position I don't have anything to lose," he said. "So I figure I might as well hand you the benefit of my observations."

Mohn smiled indulgently. He became aware of Katz's unflinching gaze and turned his attention to the Israeli commando. "Your curiosity has yet to be satisfied. Am I correct?"

"I'm interested in knowing what it is that requires such secrecy," Katz replied.

"And I had already agreed to show you—before your trained monkey went into his act," Mohn said. "So we will take up where we left off."

He reached forward and touched a button set into a small panel on his desk. A section of the right-hand wall slid aside to reveal a large television screen. A flick of another button brought a full-color image to the screen. "This video recording was made shortly before your arrival," Mohn explained. "The room you see is an isolation chamber, totally sealed off from the outside."

A door opened in the room and a man was pushed roughly inside. The door closed behind him. He was clad in dirty, bloodstained clothing. His face was swollen, battered and bloody, and he moved like a man in a great deal of pain.

"This, by the way, is Emilio Santoro. Occupation—undercover policeman. That is, until we exposed him."

Damn! Katz thought, and winced at the sight. It was too late for Farrango's courageous inside man.

"This is what my secret is all about," Mohn said.

Over the next couple of minutes Katz and Manning sat and watched in horrified silence as Emilio Santoro's terrible death was reenacted for their benefit. The concealed video camera had faithfully recorded every detail of the unfortunate cop's demise, leaving nothing to the imagination. When the recording ended and the television screen went blank, there was silence in the room.

Yakov Katzenelenbogen was the first to speak. "What in God's name was *that*?"

Mohn gestured at Neiman, who cleared his throat. "We have called it the Armageddon Virus, although it is not really a virus, but a development of the yaws bacteria, which originated in the African rain forest. It is what is known as a spirochete—a spiral bacterium. The medical jargon for it is *Treponema pertenue*. In its original form the symptoms are similar to those of congenital syphilis. By isolating the bacteria's basic structure and creating a new strain, I have accelerated the growth rate. The normal reproduction cycle of bacteria is fast. All they have to do is to grow large enough to be able to split into two, the two into four and so on. The Armageddon strain is able to do this within minutes—as the video showed. In its new form it has a high resistance to the white blood cells that normally attack any infection to the body.''

"What are you going to do? Infect the whole damn world with it?'' Manning asked in disgust.

"Not exactly,'' Mohn said. "You see, the strain can only survive for an hour or so. Then it becomes harmless. But during its life it can inflict a great deal of harm.'' The Nazi smiled. "Oh, come now, gentlemen, surely you can see its potential as a weapon of terrorism, serving to frighten and destabilize large population groups. Used in public places, it would create panic and untold suffering. And it is so easy to transport—contained in pressurized canisters no larger than a tube of toothpaste. All an operative has to do is leave it quietly concealed in some corner of an airport lounge, or a sports stadium. He sets a timer to release the bacteria after he has left. The virus does its work and then dies itself. No destruction of valuable property but a far greater body count than any bomb can achieve. And a much stronger physical impact on those who see the results.''

"So what are you going to do?" Katz asked. "Send in your Aryan murder squads in neat suits, all armed with cans of the virus?"

"Not initially," Mohn explained. "The first phase will be to sell the virus to existing terrorist groups, who will use it all over the world. It's a far safer proposition for them. No more playing about with all those unreliable explosives."

"And then?" Manning asked.

"When enough panic and fear has been spread, *we* move in. The day of the New Order will have arrived. Nazi groups in the majority of Western countries and in Europe will make a synchronized attack on seats of power. Coordinated assassinations will be carried out, and our people already in high government positions will step in and take command. In one perfectly timed operation the New Order will assume global control of all the major nations."

Manning glanced at Katz. Both Phoenix warriors had come to the same conclusion: that they were in the presence of a madman.

"Not world domination again," Katz said wearily.

"The time is ripe," Mohn snapped. His face was taut, his eyes bright—too bright.

"That's what that dickhead Hitler was always saying," Manning remarked. "Don't you guys ever give up?"

"Give up what has been preordained?" Mohn shook his head. "Never. My father brought this dream all the way from Germany. He held on to the dream until the day he died. It is my destiny to fulfill the legacy he left me.''

"Against a whole planet?" Manning asked. "This isn't 1939 all over again. Things have changed a hell of a lot."

"You think so?" Mohn sneered. "Western culture has declined. It has become soft and lazy. Indifferent. Faced by a determined enemy willing to strike at its very heart, the West will simply crumble."

"I think you've been cooped up in this damn jungle too long, pal," Manning said. "Haven't you heard about the Communist bloc? Do you think they're just going to sit back and watch you take over? Even if you could."

Mohn dismissed the suggestion with a shrug. "The Russians are no different than the Americans. They are sliding into capitalism themselves. Their satellite countries are wretched places full of discontent. My belief is that given the opportunity they would rise up against their Soviet enslavers and fight."

"To let you step in and take over?" Manning asked. "I can't believe you think that could happen."

"That's because you have no faith," Mohn replied, "no vision."

"It's because I live in the real world, pal," the Canadian said, "not on Fantasy Island."

"What do you intend to do with us?" Katz asked.

"I think you are in possession of information I need to know. You obviously take your orders from some higher authority, based in the U.S.A. I need to know how deeply your intelligence has probed my organization. Over the next few weeks there will be a great deal of activity taking place. I must know if there have been any significant leaks of information to other authorities. If you have that information I will extract it from you eventually. If you disclose it now, your deaths will be swift. If not, I promise you that life can be made extremely unpleasant. Think it over, gentlemen. You will be returned to your cell and we will speak again in the morning."

Mohn then terminated the interview, summoning guards to escort the prisoners back to their cell. Unable to speak freely because of the listening devices, the Phoenix pair spent the night getting much-needed rest.

In the morning, Katz put aside his breakfast plate and moved to where Manning was sitting. He leaned close and spoke softly in Manning's ear. "We make our move today," he whispered. "Let's play up to Mohn a little. Get him to show us around the place. He's vain enough to want to show off his project. When we see an opportunity I'll give the sign and we'll go for it."

Manning nodded. "Fine by me," he murmured.

Walking back across the cell, Katz spoke up at a normal volume. "Like it or not, Mohn certainly has this place organized well. You have to give the man credit for that."

"He'll need to be organized for what he's planning," Manning replied. "He's got to have the hardware to back it up."

"I believe he probably has," Katz said.

A couple of hours passed before a pair of armed guards came to the cell. They ushered Katz and Manning through the complex to where Mohn was talking with a couple of his black-clad Nazi fanatics.

"So, gentlemen, have you had time to think?" Mohn asked.

Manning nodded. "Maybe."

"You tell a pretty good tale, Herr Mohn," Katz said. "But do you have the muscle to back it up?"

"So you still have your doubts as to whether I'm serious. Very well, gentlemen. Follow me."

During the hour that followed Kurt Mohn guided Katz and Manning on a tour of his base. The upper level contained communications and administration offices and facilities. Also on that floor were the laboratories and the isolation rooms. One section housed a sick bay, complete with its own operating room. There was a lot of sophisticated computer hardware, up-to-date radio and electronics equipment and a photographic and video department. On the floor below were recreation facilities, common rooms and dormitories. Each dormitory had its own toilets and fully equipped shower room. For the higher ranks there were also individual sleeping quarters similar to luxury hotel suites. Also on that level were a large kitchen and dining area.

The most interesting area to the Phoenix commandos was the basement. There, apart from the cells where they had been held, were large storage rooms, each a self-contained unit that could be closed off by heavy steel doors. The rooms held vast stores of equipment that ranged from uniforms to weapons, and everything in between: medical supplies, boxed and canned rations, even a large vault that contained hard cash, the revenues from Mohn's drug operation. The drug production section was also housed in the basement area, the whole setup based in one large corner, with all the latest equipment for refining and processing cocaine.

"As you can see," Mohn said with undisguised pride, "nothing has been left to chance."

They were walking along one of the connecting hallways, with Mohn leading the way. Katz was beside the Nazi, Manning a few steps back. The two armed guards followed close behind.

"I'm impressed," Katz said. "I may question your motives but I have to admire your precision."

"Any project requires sound organization in order to succeed," Mohn acknowledged.

"I'd call it teutonic thoroughness," Manning said.

"If you wish," Mohn agreed. "There is nothing wrong with being thorough."

He guided them through a door into a well-equipped gym, where a couple dozen of his men were performing rigorous exercises.

"I have fitness experts to train my men. Martial arts instructors, men who can teach them all the combat techniques they will need. Plus demolition and sabotage experts. We have them all."

Mohn led his Phoenix prisoners farther down the hall to a steel door and pressed a button to open it. They walked into an armory. Racks of weapons were stored along the walls, as well as crates of more weapons: grenades, packs of C-4 plastique explosive and ammunition for every type of weapon. Deeper in the room was a firing range. For safety Mohn closed the steel door, shutting off their party from the rest of the basement.

"Still, even with highly trained personnel, the power of the gun is very important," he said. "Don't you think so?" He turned away from his captives to survey his lethal resources. His eyes blazed with that fanatical light that has meant misery for so many over the decades.

Katz smiled. "Oh, yes, I must agree with you there, Herr Mohn." As he spoke he gave the merest nod in Gary Manning's direction.

As the Canadian acknowledged Katz's signal, he exploded into action, half turning toward the black-clad flunky on his left. The Nazi, off guard after the long tour around the complex, had left his reflexes in his locker. He barely had time to register Manning's move before the Canadian's fist smashed into the side of his face. Bone disintegrated under the impact and the guard's head snapped to one side, blood flying from his gaping mouth. Manning followed up with a second punch that caught the stunned guy in the stomach. Grunting in agony, the Nazi doubled over. Manning kneed him full in the face, reducing the guy's features to a scarlet puree.

The second he had signaled Manning, Katz made his own move. His artificial forearm and hand and his slightly paunchy appearance often worked in his favor, causing enemies to underestimate his capabilities. Katz was no slouch; when the time came he could *move*. He executed an extremely fast move now, as his right arm lashed up at the face of the armed guard standing beside him. The steel tips of Katz's prosthesis jabbed deep into the guard's left eye, popping the orb from its socket in a welter of bloody fluid.

The guard screamed as burning pain engulfed his ruined eye socket. He abandoned any thoughts of the promised New Order and concentrated on his own personal agony. The weapon he was carrying slipped from his fingers as he clapped both hands over the gory hole in his face.

Katz caught the SMG as it fell. He braced it across his right arm, swinging the Uzi in Mohn's direction. A moment later Manning did the same thing with the weapon he had retrieved from his disabled guard.

Mohn had backed away, coming to a stop as he banged up against the armory's steel door. "Do you think you can get away with this?" the Nazi leader fumed.

Manning grinned. "We're doing pretty well up to now."

Mohn stiffened, drawing his shoulders back. "But you are trapped. Surrounded by my storm troopers. You will never get out."

"Don't bet your Iron Cross on it, Herr Mohn," Manning said. He stepped up to the Nazi and relieved him of the holstered automatic pistol he carried.

"See if you can locate the weapons they took from us," Katz said, positioning himself so he could keep a close watch on Mohn and the two disabled guards.

"Here they are," Manning called a few minutes later. He had been walking up and down the racks of weapons. Now he returned, carrying Katz's Uzi and SIG-Sauer P-226. He also had the Phoenix commando's combat harness, its pouches still containing extra ammunition for Katz's weapons. Over his other arm Manning had his own harness. He had already donned the shoulder rig that held his .357 Desert Eagle. Over his shoulder hung his FN-FAL assault rifle and the backup SA80 he'd brought along.

When both Phoenix warriors were fully armed with their own weapons they added extra firepower to their personal arsenals. They secured two leather satchels each to their belts, into which they placed as many fragmentation grenades as they could carry, as well as additional magazines for their weapons; Manning had located plenty of 5.56 mm mags that would fit the SA80, as well as 9 mm for Katz's Uzi.

"All set," Manning said.

Mohn stared at the Phoenix pair. "You are both mad," he exclaimed. "You will never leave this complex alive."

Prodding the self-styled führer in the stomach with the barrel of his Uzi, Katz said, "On the floor, and do it now."

Mohn hesitated, still sure of his invincibility. That sureness crumbled when Katz clipped him across the jaw with the barrel of the Uzi. Mohn gasped, felt warm blood running down his chin.

"That was for Emilio Santoro," the Phoenix pro said. "I wonder how many more poor bastards have died the same way to help you perfect your damned Armageddon Virus? And you want to run the world? God help us all. I think we're better off the way we are."

"You will not stop us," Mohn yelled, his voice rising to an insane scream. "We were betrayed last time. Adolf Hitler would have succeeded if he had not been surrounded by traitors and cowards."

"No," Katz said. "He failed because he was a raving madman who wanted to infect the world with his twisted beliefs. He was stopped because there is a kind of divine justice that sometimes intervenes. Hitler failed, and you crazed fanatics will always fail, because good, honest people won't let you carry your mad dreams into reality. They'll fight back and they'll win."

"Now get down on that floor, pal, before I put you there," Gary Manning said.

Mohn did as he was told this time. Stripping the belt from one of the semiconscious guards, Manning tied the Nazi's hands behind his back.

"Did you find any timing devices among the explosives?" Katz asked.

"Yeah," Manning replied.

"Set a few," Katz said. "One way or another I want this place to go up."

Manning grinned. "I'll set them for thirty minutes."

"If we're not out of this place by then we never will be," Katz said.

Neither Phoenix fighter relished the idea of dying, but they were practical men, and knew they were not invincible. Every member of Phoenix Force accepted that his next mission could be his last. Death favored no one, good or bad, clean or dirty. The shadow of death stalked them all, and one day death would reach out with its bony hand to claim the soul of another individual whose life span had expired. When that time came there was no escape. Death allowed no options. No alternatives. It was strictly a one-way ticket. Each time the force set out on a mission, they all walked a line that was becoming progressively thinner, pushing luck to its limits. Not that they escaped without injury. Every one of them had been wounded, and they all carried the scars of their close encounters with death. As time passed they all recognized their physical vulnerability, and they also carried the mental strain of their profession around with them day and night.

Yet every time the call for help went out to Stony Man, they responded without hesitation, often plunging into a mission after scarcely time to recover from the previous one. Hal Brognola, the man who directed their operations, regularly found himself racked with guilt at having to send the five-man team out on yet another dangerous assignment. He knew the thin line they walked each time they stepped into the killing grounds. He respected the bravery of these unsung heroes, men who fought the dirty battles for the free world and never even received recognition. Phoenix Force and Able Team did their jobs because of an honest love for freedom and the right of decent people to live their lives the way they wanted, out from under the heel of tyranny, free from the grip of the dictator, not terrorized by the criminal element and its sleazy world of drugs and corruption.

If they had required any acknowledgment of their achievements, the Phoenix commandos would have been content with a quick nod from the man who had started the whole Phoenix concept: Mack Bolan.

Bolan was the lone crusader who had pitched in against the Mafia when the whole of officialdom had stood around helpless. The destruction of his beloved family had catapulted the soldier from Vietnam headlong into another war. At first, this war was personal, but as time went on and Bolan's crusade took on epic proportions, his everlasting war became a battle on behalf of mankind itself. Bolan's direct justice aimed itself at every individual and organization that attempted to inflict harm on the innocents of the world. Whether they were Cosa Nostra, KGB, terrorists or purveyors of child pornography, the breed known as Animal Man could never rid itself of the Executioner's shadow, which followed and struck without mercy. Bolan's total dedication touched others, and through his influence the Phoenix program was created. The men of Phoenix Force and Able Team all shared his vision.

Both Katz and Manning knew what Mack Bolan's response would have been in their position. The possibility of death would have served only to spur him on—to pit his life against overwhelming odds in order to strike out against the forces of evil.

It took Gary Manning no more than five minutes to rig the explosive devices. He set the central timer that would blow all the individual packs of C-4 and returned to where Katz was waiting by the armory door. "Okay," Manning said. "Let's go kick some Nazi ass."

"Get them on their feet," Katz said. "We'll take them out with us, then close the door and disable the lock. After that they're on their own."

Manning couldn't resist a grin. "And so are we!"

Katz's reply was to thumb the button that opened the steel door.

17

The moment the door opened enough to allow a man to pass through the gap, Katz gave Kurt Mohn a hefty shove, propelling the Nazi across the corridor. Then he turned and caught hold of the collar of one of the guards and assisted him out of the armory. Manning did the same with the remaining guard.

Katz stepped out into the corridor, which was momentarily deserted. As Manning followed, he thumbed the button that activated the closing mechanism of the armory door, and the heavy steel barrier began its return journey. This time it seemed to take forever.

Kurt Mohn, having recovered his balance, glanced up and down the hall. He cursed wildly when he realized there was no one around to help. The Nazi leader did not give up easily. He lifted his head and began to yell at the top of his voice.

"That son of a bitch is starting to get on my nerves," Manning muttered. He took three long strides across the passage and laid Mohn out on the floor with a single swipe from the butt of his FAL.

The armory door locked into place with a solid thud. Katz motioned Manning to stand clear, then raised his Uzi and shot the operating mechanism to shreds. "That should keep them out for a while," he said.

"And those shots are going to bring the bad guys on the run," Manning pointed out.

"We'll head for the cell area. I have a feeling there must be others locked up there. If we can free them, they could help us."

They moved out at a steady pace along opposite sides of the corridor. They had barely moved ten yards before armed figures rounded a bend ahead of them. Harsh commands were rapped out in German.

Manning countered those commands with a deadly burst from his FAL, 7.62 slugs seeking soft bodies. Men went down yelling, blood spurting from lacerated flesh, shards of splintered bone protruding from pulpy wounds.

The Canadian's initial burst of fire gave Katz the opportunity to pull a grenade from the satchel he was wearing. Pulling the pin, the Israeli counted off three seconds then hurled the grenade into the midst of the Nazis.

The grenade exploded with a thunderous crash, filling the passage with smoke and a brilliant flash. A rain of dust and concrete debris blasted along the hall, carrying with it severed limbs and chunks of bloody flesh and bone.

Katz and Manning moved on, bypassing the scattered corpses, until they reached the first intersection of the corridors that crisscrossed the basement area.

Katz pointed to one of the branch hallways. "That one leads to the cell area."

"I'll cover you," Manning said.

Katz nodded and broke away from the scant protection of the wall, dashing across the empty space, heading for the next corridor.

A scuffling sound came from one of the other corridors, and a pair of armed Nazis, clad in black uniforms, appeared.

Manning spotted them the moment they showed their faces. He arced the FAL's muzzle around and triggered a short burst that caught the closest thug in the chest and throat, spinning him around and banging him face first against the wall. The Nazi rolled along the wall, terrible gurgling sounds coming from his lacerated, bloody throat. He was clawing at the gaping, ragged wound with his fingers, as if trying to stop the pain and the gushing blood.

The second Nazi ducked low when Manning's shots took out his partner. He ran forward at a crouch, pausing long enough to loose off a volley of shots from his Uzi that drove the Canadian back into cover, chips of concrete peppering his face.

In the meantime Katz had reached the corridor he was aiming for. He turned and blasted the second Nazi himself. His Uzi chattered loudly, sending a stream of 9 mm flesh-shredders into the fanatic's torso. The Nazi gave a startled yell as the slugs slammed him off his feet. He hit the floor and made a tremendous effort to rise to his feet again. The struggle caused him to cough up gouts of blood from his punctured lungs, and he sank back to the concrete to die.

"Gary, you all right?" Katz called anxiously.

The Canadian stepped into view, nodding. His face was streaked with blood where concrete splinters had cut him, but he was otherwise unharmed. "I'm on my way," he said as he joined Katz.

Just as Katz and Manning stepped along the hall that led to the cells, a heavy burst of firing from one of the other corridors threw a hail of slugs at them. The Phoenix pair hit the floor as the firing continued for long seconds. Bullets hit the walls and the ceiling around them, showering them with dust and fragments of concrete.

Rolling on his side, Manning pulled a couple of grenades from his satchel. He popped the pins and released the levers, then lobbed the grenades back the way they had come. The first explosion was followed a moment later by the second. The din of the grenades was accompanied by yells of rage and some of pain.

Katz and Manning scrambled to their feet again and ran down the hall. Ahead of them more Nazi fanatics burst into view from a doorway. Autofire once more filled the corridor with hot slugs.

Flattening himself against the wall, Manning leveled his FAL, triggering accurate bursts that cut a pair of the self-styled Aryan supermen down to size. Hot 7.62 steel-jackets cored through flesh, seeking bone to splinter and organs to puncture. The New Order elite died just as had the Nazi scum of the Hitler regime, with blood spurting from their bodies and their limbs twitching in a grotesque dance of death.

Resting his Uzi across his prosthesis, Yakov Katzenelenbogen displayed the calm and deliberation that had brought him through countless moments of personal danger. He always worked on the principle that the quickest to fire were usually those who ended up dead. In combat speed wasn't always entirely desirable. Any fool could pull a trigger and spray an area with bullets. The important thing was to hit the target, and that took a little more time. Katz frequently proved his point by taking a fraction of a second longer to aim than another man might, ensuring he had his targets locked in his sights before he touched the Uzi's trigger.

Three of Mohn's goons served now to demonstrate Katz's principle. The first caught three 9 mm slugs through his chest straight to his heart, turning that wondrous organ to mush. Before pain even had time to register on the Nazi's face, the trio of slugs emerged between his shoulders in a minigeyser of minced flesh, bone and blood.

Katz's second burst hit slightly higher because the chosen target decided, at the last moment, to duck— hoping to avoid being shot. His move brought him directly in line with Katz's 9 mm volley. The entire burst took him in the head, impacting to the left of his nose. His eye vanished in a blossom of red. The cluster of slugs caved his face in, disintegrating bone and muscle. They continued on through the skull, opening it up like an overripe melon being whacked with a baseball bat. The Nazi was thrown back by the impact, bouncing off the corridor wall at his back, where he left a large percentage of the contents of his skull. Gobs of bloody flesh and brains stuck to the concrete there.

Adjusting his aim, Katz took out the third target with a well-placed burst that struck directly over the guy's belt buckle. Dropping his weapon, the Nazi grabbed at his middle, moaning in agony as rods of red-hot iron cored deep into his torso. He sank to his knees, his chin dropping to his chest, where he could see thick streams of blood pumping out between his fingers. After long seconds he sank to the floor and curled up in a fetal ball.

By that time Katz and Manning had moved on, scouring the way ahead with a couple of grenades. They reached the cell area without encountering further opposition.

While Manning took up a watching stance, Katz checked out the cells. He found a central control panel whose buttons opened or closed the cell doors. Doors could be opened individually or all at once. Katz chose the latter option. He activated the buttons and heard the muted sound of the bolts being drawn.

Making his way along the line of doors, Katz pulled them open and peered inside. Most of the cells were occupied. The wide-eyed Indians, from local tribes, stared at the Israeli in astonishment.

"You are free," he said. The captives just continued staring.

"Free!" Katz wished he knew their language. In desperation he reverted to Portuguese. *"Livre! Livre!"* He was pleased he'd picked up a smattering of the language.

The word was understood at last. One Indian pushed his way to the front of the cell. He jabbered excitedly in what was plainly his own tongue, then glanced at Katz. *"Livre?"* he asked.

Katz nodded. *"Sim."* He moved along the line of cells, doing his best to draw the captives out, aware all the time that Mohn's Nazi thugs could appear at any moment.

"Anyone understand English?" he kept asking.

"I do," a voice answered.

A lean, dark Indian stepped from one of the cells. He was gaunt, almost emaciated, and his body, clad only in a pair of soiled, bloodstained cotton pants, showed the signs of recent harsh treatment.

"Who are you?" the Indian asked.

"Friends," Katz said. "We're here to put Mohn out of business. But there is no time to explain it all to you. Tell your companions they are free. But in about a half hour explosives will go off and destroy much of this place. You must get out before then if you can. We can do no more than free you from your cells. The rest is up to you."

The Indian translated for the rest of his group. An angry murmur arose.

"They want vengeance for what these men have done to us," the young Indian explained. "Many of our people have died in the white rooms. Killed by the sickness created by these blackshirts."

"Mohn's people are armed. You have no weapons," Katz pointed out.

The Indian smiled. "Then we will get weapons."

Manning gave a low whistle to attract Katz's attention. "We've got company coming," he advised.

Katz slotted a fresh magazine into his Uzi, drawing back the bolt to cock the weapon.

The thump of combat boots against concrete signaled the approach of more Nazi troops. They burst into view around the bend of one of the approach corridors and spread out when they saw the gathered Indians.

"Find cover!" Katz yelled.

Even as the English speaking Indian began to translate, a number of Nazi guns opened fire. A deadly hail of slugs whiplashed through the air, catching some of the slower Indians before they could clear the area. Blood-streaked brown bodies tumbled to the concrete, twitching and writhing in agony as their nervous systems reacted to the impact of high-velocity bullets.

Manning had taken cover behind a sloping concrete buttress, and from there he returned fire, his FAL spitting 7.62 manglers that found their mark in tender flesh.

Ducking behind one of the open cell doors, Katz let loose with his Uzi, his first blast catching one reckless fanatic who had decided to try for a closer position. The stream of 9 mm sizzlers chopped the Nazi goon's legs from under him, reducing his lower limbs to shredded meat. The thug crashed to the floor in a screaming heap, losing his weapon. He tried to drag himself back to his companions, his useless legs trailing behind him. Twin smears of blood marked his progress.

Despite the heavy crisscross of gunfire, one of the Indians made an attempt to retrieve the weapon the Nazi had dropped. He got to within three feet before he was blown off his feet by the concentrated firepower of at least four of the Nazi guns. Dead on his feet, the Indian was smashed brutally to the concrete.

Not wanting to get pinned down, Katz plucked another grenade from his satchel and lobbed it toward the mouth of the hallway that concealed the main body of Nazis. As the fragmentation grenade dropped in among them, the Nazi thugs broke and scattered. Some ran toward the cell area, directly into the line of fire commanded by Katz and Manning. The Phoenix pair opened fire and eliminated the Nazis before they could unleash any fire of their own. Bullet-blasted bodies were hurled into oblivion by the accurate, unrelenting autofire coming from the weapons of the Phoenix warriors.

The detonating grenade filled the area with smoke and debris—human and otherwise. The echoing rattle of the blast was punctuated by the screams of the injured and dying.

"You wanted weapons," Katz said to the English-speaking Indian.

"There they are. Take them if you must. Just remember what I told you about the explosives we set."

The Indian nodded and spoke to his companions. The excited Indians surged toward the downed Nazis, searching for abandoned weapons.

"Well?" Manning asked.

"I'd like to get up to the laboratory," Katz said. "That virus needs destroying."

Manning sighed with resignation. "I had a feeling you were going to say something like that."

"I'd hate to disappoint you," the Israeli replied with a sudden grin.

The pair turned and took the corridor that would lead them to the elevator. They found the elevator unguarded. When Manning touched the door button, the elevator opened immediately and the Phoenix pair stepped inside. Katz thumbed the button for the desired floor, and the elevator doors closed and it began to rise.

Manning took advantage of the brief respite to exchange his FAL for the SA80. The SA80's shorter length would give him an advantage in the close-quarter situation they were in. The long barrel of the FAL could be restrictive in cramped areas. He flicked the fire selector on the SA80 to automatic. The FAL went over his back, held in place by its sling.

The elevator jerked to a stop. Katz and Manning stood to either side of the doors as they slid open. Silence greeted them, beckoned them to step out. They almost did so, then Katz glanced across at Manning. The Canadian shook his head. Something wasn't quite right.

Katz took out a grenade and pulled the pin. He popped the lever and held the grenade for a count of three. Then he tossed it out of the elevator. It hit the floor with a distinct thud. In that same moment a man yelled in abject terror. Someone else shouted in German.

The elevator rocked as the shock waves from the exploding grenade reached it. Tendrils of smoke drifted through the open door. Something landed at Katz's feet with a sodden sound. It was a human hand, blood still flowing from the severed stump of wrist.

The Phoenix warriors ducked low and exited the elevator, weapons at the ready.

Three dead Nazi troopers lay sprawled on the floor of the corridor, black uniforms tattered and stained with fresh blood. They had caught the full blast of the fragmentation grenade at close quarters. Coils of blue-gray intestines were still oozing from the opened torso of one corpse.

Katz and Manning sprinted along the hall, making for the double doors at the far end. Behind those doors lay the laboratory where they had first met Kurt Mohn.

Reaching the doors, the Phoenix commandos used their boots to kick them open. As they barreled into the lab they saw two people.

One was Otto Neiman. The other was a uniformed Nazi trooper, carrying a Heckler and Koch MP-5.

The Nazi was facing the doors as they burst open. He caught a glimpse of the Phoenix pair as they erupted into the lab, but was then thrown into confusion as the two parted company, Katz breaking to the left and Manning to the right. The Nazi had to make a decision—which of the intruders to tackle first.

He waited too long, and the choice was taken from him. Gary Manning's SA80 settled on target and spit out a stream of 5.56 mm death-dealers that all but severed the fanatic's head from his shoulders. Twitching from top to toe, the Nazi's lacerated neck sprayed a mist of blood as he stumbled back against one of the workbenches. His flailing arms sent glass beakers and tubes crashing to the floor. Still twitching, the dead Nazi hit the floor himself, fingers of blood running out from his shredded neck.

Otto Neiman made a half-hearted dash for the door at his back, clawing for the Walther PPK he carried in a shoulder holster beneath his white lab coat.

Katz drew his SIG-Sauer P-226 and calmly put a 9 mm bullet through Neiman's left shoulder. The force of the bullet slammed the scientist against the door, shattering the frosted-glass upper panel. The German almost fell through the door. He struggled to regain his balance, gasping with pain as broken shards of glass gouged his face and upper body.

Katz stepped up from behind the Nazi. He used his steel prosthesis to hook Neiman's gun from its holster and toss it across the room. Then he pulled Neiman around to face him. The German's face was ashen, streaked with blood that flowed freely from the deep cuts caused by the broken glass. Where Katz's bullet had emerged from Neiman's shoulder there was a protruding, pulpy mass of bleeding flesh.

"Herr Neiman," Katz said. "Surely you weren't leaving?"

Any arrogance Neiman might have displayed previously had fled. He was a frightened, injured man who wanted nothing more than to be left alone. He made no attempt to reply to Katz's question. His skeletal face began to glisten with perspiration, the pockmarks in his flesh becoming discolored, giving him a blotchy appearance.

"Where is the Armageddon Virus stored?" Katz asked sternly, sensing Neiman's crumbling personality.

"At the other end of the building," Neiman answered dully.

"What about formulations?" Manning demanded. "You must have those recorded."

The Nazi nodded weakly, gesturing over his shoulder in the direction of the door with the broken glass panel. "In there. All the data is stored on computer disks."

"Stay here," Katz said to Manning.

The Canadian nodded, watching as Katz pushed Neiman toward the computer room.

Inside the room an air conditioner hummed softly, maintaining a steady atmosphere. There were a number of computer work stations, each with its own monitor screen and keyboard. Only one was operational, the screen glowing softly.

"Where are the disks?" Katz demanded.

Swaying slightly, Neiman indicated a metal box that resembled a filing cabinet in miniature.

"In there."

"Open it."

Neiman fished a key from his pocket. He unlocked the box and slid out the tray that was fixed inside. Neatly racked in the tray were the plastic casings that enclosed the computer disks. Katz counted an even dozen.

"Are there any more?" he demanded. "Backup copies?"

"Everything is there," Neiman assured the Phoenix commander. "Six master disks and six copies. They are all quite safe. It is not as easy to erase a disk as some people think it is."

Katz took the disks and dropped them in one of his pockets. He motioned Neiman out of the room. Turning back to the computer setup, Katz swept all the machines off the bench tops, allowing them to smash on the floor.

Back in the lab, Katz dumped the computer disks in a stainless-steel sink that was fitted in one corner of the room. He searched the lab shelves until he found a bottle of industrial alcohol, which he emptied over the disks.

"Matches? Lighter?" he demanded.

Neiman pointed to one of the drawers. Yanking it open, Katz found a lighter. He flicked the wheel, thumbing the flame control to maximum. Then he lowered the lighter into the sink. The alcohol ignited with a dull thud, bright flame filling the sink. The heat melted the plastic casings of the computer disks, exposing and destroying the fragile recording disks inside. As the temperature rose, the plastic itself began to burn, giving off thick, noxious smoke.

"Now show us where the virus is being stored," Katz said, pushing Neiman toward the door.

As they reentered the corridor, Neiman turning them in the direction of the far end of the building, they heard distant gunfire. Accompanying the shooting were wild, primitive yells.

"Sounds like our Indian allies have the same idea," Manning said.

"The natives?" Neiman asked. "They are free?"

Katz nodded.

"Mein Gott!" Neiman exclaimed. "If they reach the virus and expose it..."

"Oh, great," Manning said.

Katz glanced at him. "Is that the best you can do?" he asked.

"Oh, fucking great," Manning expanded.

"Couldn't have said it better myself," Katz acknowledged. "Now let's move."

18

"So who said it had to be fair?" Rafael Encizo asked.

McCarter turned away from Louis Farrango's corpse and fixed his gaze on Jorgio Cavantes. The faithless informer shrank away from the British commando's cold, bitter eyes.

"You miserable little bastard!" McCarter said. He didn't shout, or even raise his voice. His words were delivered in a flat, soulless monotone. "Another good man dead. And you killed him, Cavantes. I'm going to enjoy slicing you into little pieces." The Phoenix pro closed his fist over the handle of the Predator.

"You cannot do this," Cavantes protested.

Grimaldi, standing behind Cavantes, cleared his throat. "If he sets his mind to it he can do anything," he said.

Encizo nodded. "Looks to me like he's already made up his mind."

"If you kill me I cannot tell you what you want to know," Cavantes said suddenly, grasping at straws.

McCarter loosened his grip on the Predator now. "What makes you think you have anything we want?"

"The location of Mohn's base," Cavantes offered.

McCarter feigned indifference.

Sweating heavily, Cavantes turned to Encizo. "If you knew where it was, you could free your comrades."

"Makes no difference if they're already dead," McCarter said icily.

Cavantes rubbed a trembling hand across his glistening face. "I do not wish to die," he said.

McCarter's anger broke through. He lunged at the terrified double agent, grabbing him by the front of his dirty shirt. Shoving the man to his knees, McCarter thrust Cavantes toward the bloodied, violated corpse of Louis Farrango.

"Neither did he," the Brit thundered. "But it didn't save him."

Tears sprang into Cavantes's eyes, tears of sheer terror. He was certain McCarter was about to plunge the knife into his throat. "Please...do not kill me...I will guide you to Mohn's base."

"Like the last time?" Encizo reminded him.

Cavantes shook his head. He held up a shaking hand. "This time I *will* take you there. I swear on my life."

"Remember that, chum," McCarter growled, "because that's how it's going to be. I'm going to be beside you all the way. If I even smell something not right, you'll be the first to die."

"We ready to go then?" Grimaldi asked quietly.

McCarter nodded.

"What about Louis?" Encizo asked.

McCarter glanced at Grimaldi. "When we get in the air burn this place to the ground. It's a cleaner way to go than being put in a hole and covered with dirt."

They exited the building and made their way to Dragon Slayer. As Grimaldi fired up the combat chopper, with Encizo seated in the copilot's seat, McCarter bundled Cavantes in the rear compartment and used riot cuffs to secure him. Dragon Slayer rose into the air smoothly, hovering over the settlement.

"Disable that other chopper, too," Encizo said.

Grimaldi nodded and eased Dragon Slayer around. He touched the armaments control panel, selecting the weaponry he wanted. A light touch of the firing button sent an HE rocket whooshing down at the Bell helicopter that had brought the secret-service goons to the settlement. The Bell went up in a ball of orange-and-yellow flame, scattering debris across a wide area. Pulling back, Grimaldi then selected white-phosphorous rockets. He laid a pair of them in the main building. The rockets exploded in a rain of shimmering white that rapidly expanded into a blazing inferno. Within five minutes the entire building was ablaze, great tongues of fire bursting from every window.

"Let's go," McCarter said, tapping Grimaldi on the shoulder.

The ace pilot nodded and spun Dragon Slayer on to its new course, the same one he'd used coming in, which was now locked into Dragon Slayer's computer. Once they reached the point where Grimaldi had picked up McCarter and Encizo, it would be up to Cavantes to guide them the rest of the way to Kurt Mohn's secret base.

Grimaldi pushed Dragon Slayer to the limit. The sleek combat ship hurtled across the Amazon landscape, the jungle nothing more than a green blur beneath.

"Watch out for that Hind," McCarter said. "It was going to come back and pick up those creeps who stayed behind to look for us. If the chopper crew can't spot them they may decide to take a look around."

Exactly twenty minutes later Grimaldi sighted a dark spot on the horizon. He watched it grow and take shape, and then smiled. "Here comes your Hind," he said.

At that moment the Russian-built gunship picked up Dragon Slayer's presence, and banked sharply, gaining height.

"Can't you do better than that?" Grimaldi asked, grinning at the Hind's antics.

"He's a big bugger," McCarter observed.

"No fun taking on a little one," Grimaldi pointed out. He made swift alterations to Dragon Slayer's flight path, flinging the combat helicopter around the sky like a jet fighter. Grimaldi was in no mood to play games. He was aware, as were McCarter and Encizo, that they had no time to waste.

The pilot of the Hind abruptly found he was the pursued, not the pursuer. He made frantic attempts at losing Dragon Slayer, but the sleek combat machine clung to his tail. Finally, Grimaldi loosed off a single, heat-seeking missile that homed in on the Hind's hot engine and blew the Soviet-made machine out of the sky.

Checking his computer readout a few minutes later, Grimaldi said, "This is where I picked you guys up last night."

McCarter nudged Cavantes, who had remained silent and withdrawn throughout the flight. "No crap," the cockney hardman warned. "Just point the way."

"Hold it!" Encizo said. He was pointing off to their left. "There was an explosion. I saw the flash."

Peering through one of the side windows, McCarter said, "I see it. Smoke rising over the trees."

"What do we do?" Grimaldi asked. "Ignore it? Check it out?"

"It could be one of the guys," McCarter pointed out. "We have to be sure."

"I agree," Encizo said. "Take us in."

Grimaldi turned Dragon Slayer, swooping in toward the rising spiral of smoke.

As they drifted through the smoke, their eyes scanning the terrain, the first thing they saw was the burning wreckage of a helicopter in a wide clearing. Just beyond the wreckage was a large pool of still water.

It was Encizo who suddenly gave a whoop of joy. He pointed groundward. "Would you believe it if you hadn't seen it with your own eyes?"

There, emerging from the cover of the dense jungle, was the familiar figure of Calvin James. He was carrying a Kalashnikov AK-47 in one hand and waving wildly with the other.

"Here we go," Grimaldi said, and took Dragon Slayer in for a feather-light landing. He broke the seal on the side hatch, and moments later James's grinning face appeared in the opening.

The Phoenix team greeted one another enthusiastically.

"Took your time getting back here," James said.

McCarter scowled. "We reckoned you'd be having so much fun we decided not to spoil it."

"All depends on what you call fun," James retorted.

By this time Dragon Slayer had become airborne again, and Grimaldi was waiting impatiently for his new course. McCarter got Encizo to trade seats with Cavantes so that he could direct Grimaldi.

McCarter, Encizo and James retreated to the rear compartment to have a council of war, bringing one another up to date with the events of the past couple of days.

"I'm really sorry about Louis," James said. "He was a hell of a good guy."

"Well, let's just hope we don't have to start saying things like that about Katz and Gary," McCarter snapped. "I want those two out of that place alive and kicking."

James detailed what he had seen at the base, not forgetting to include information about the rest of Mohn's fleet of helicopters. "There are a lot of weapons around the place,'' added the Chicago tough guy. ''The only consolation is that, though they're supposed to be well-trained, Mohn's combat teams don't appear to have had much in the way of actual battle experience.''

''Tough on them,'' McCarter observed. ''They'll damn well get some when we hit town.''

''Hey, guys,'' Grimaldi called. ''According to Cavantes we should pick up the base in about thirty minutes.''

''Ho-hum,'' McCarter said, ''here we go again.''

''Time to load for bear,'' Encizo said.

''Not bear,'' James corrected him. ''Capybara.''

''What the hell is that?'' McCarter asked.

James grinned. ''Amazon jungle rats,'' he said. ''Big, black, Nazi rats.''

19

White-coated laboratory technicians rushed past Katz and Manning. They ignored the Phoenix warriors. There was panic in their actions, and even though they were yelling in German, it was evident that something had caused them to run scared.

Without pausing, Katz nudged Otto Neiman. "What are they saying?" the Israeli demanded.

Neiman turned his sweating gray face toward the Phoenix commander. "The Indians you freed. They have forced their way into the storage facility. They are destroying everything. If they damage the containers holding the Armageddon Virus, it could spread through the whole building."

"I don't blame them for what they're doing," Katz said, "but I hope they don't find the virus."

Double doors blocked their way, but as they reached them, the doors burst open. A lab technician hurried past them, leaving a lone armed guard facing the Phoenix pair.

The Nazi struck out with the SMG he was carrying, the hard butt just creasing the top of Katz's left shoulder. Katz ducked low, under the guard's weapon, and rammed his Uzi up between the Nazi's legs. The guy uttered a shrill cry of agony. Continuing his action, Katz pushed his shoulder against the Nazi thug's stomach, knocking him off balance. He staggered back, banging up against the wall.

"Keep going," Katz snapped at Manning, and moved in on the dazed guard.

Swearing violently in German, the blond fanatic aimed a heavy boot at Katz. The Israeli dodged the blow easily. Still cursing, the Nazi lashed out with his SMG. The barrel clanged against the steel of Katz's prosthesis. Before the guard could withdraw the weapon, Katz snapped the jaws of his prosthesis shut over the barrel, forcing it up out of the way. He swung up the Uzi he held in his left hand and touched the trigger, sending a stream of 9 mm slugs into and through the guard's chest. A startled cry burst from the thug's open mouth as the 9 mm thrashers cored their way into his body, penetrating and destroying lungs and heart before severing the spinal column and then emerging. The guard collapsed, all feeling gone from his lower limbs. He flopped loosely on the floor, leaving a glistening trail of bloody gore smeared down the wall.

Katz turned and pushed through the doors. Manning and Neiman were halfway along that part of the hallway. At the far end the corridor opened up into a wider area, which terminated at a glass-paneled wall. Clustered around this area were most of the Indians

Katz had freed from the cells. Three bloody, lifeless black-clad Nazi guards lay sprawled on the floor.

Reaching the cluster of excited Indians, Katz shoved his way through until he spotted the one who spoke English.

The Indian gave a triumphant smile when he recognized Katz. "Here is where they keep the silent death," the Indian said.

Through the window fronting the storage facility, Katz saw that half a dozen Indians were ransacking the room, tossing aside anything they could lay their hands on.

"Stop them," Katz urged.

"Why?" the Indian asked.

"If they damage the containers holding the virus—the silent death—they'll release it and we could all die."

The Indian hesitated, unsure.

Then Otto Neiman gave a hysterical cry. He lunged toward the glass, his skeletal hands waving before him. "Too late! Too late!" he moaned.

Katz turned, peering through the glass. One of the Indians had smashed open a metal locker and had dragged out thin aluminum canisters, which he was methodically battering against the side of the locker before casting them aside.

"The virus?" Katz asked.

Neiman nodded.

Pushing his way past the Indians bunched at the door to the room, Katz grabbed the handle of the open door and pulled it shut, dropping the locking bar into place.

"Why do you lock the door?" demanded the English-speaking Indian.

"They have allowed the virus to escape," Katz said. "If it gets beyond that room you will all be infected and die. You must get your men away from here. Now."

"Look," Neiman said.

The virus had begun to attack the Indians in the storage room. The six unfortunate men were already reacting to the infection, scratching at their exposed flesh. One rubbed his throat, eyes bulging. Another stared in horror at the flesh of his arm as it began to undergo a change.

"Go!" Katz said. "Get out of this place now!"

"Can those men get out of there at all?" Manning asked.

Neiman shook his head. "The door can only be opened from the outside. The glass is armored and bulletproof."

"Then hopefully we can contain the virus," Katz said.

"Not much consolation for those poor bastards," Manning said.

"So they must die?" the Indian asked.

Katz nodded. "I'm sorry, my friend, but we can do nothing for them."

The Indian glanced at Neiman. The German was leaning against the wall of the passage, one hand clutched to the bloody wound in his shoulder. Sweat was pouring down his haggard face.

"He is the one," the Indian said. "He made the silent death. So he must die also."

Before anyone could stop him the Indian raised the AK-47 he held in his hands and pulled the trigger. He held it down until the magazine of the Kalashnikov had been emptied into Otto Neiman's lean body. The stream of 7.62 mm slugs shredded the German, punching him hard against the wall and holding him there as they chewed his flesh and bone to bloody tatters. His chest caved in under the impact of the slugs, which exploded through his back in a splatter of glistening gore and hammered into the wall. As the muzzle of the AK-47 rose, 7.62s stitched Neiman's upper chest and throat. The flesh opened and his blood splashed across the floor. When the Kalashnikov clicked empty, the Indian watched impassively as Neiman's ragged, bleeding body slithered wetly down the wall to curl up in a twitching heap on the floor.

"Now we go," the Indian said.

He spoke to his companions. The Indians withdrew silently, scattering along the passage, leaving Katz and Manning alone outside the locked room.

The Canadian took a long look through the armored glass at the wretched creatures who were dying horribly before his eyes. He glanced at Katz. The Israeli's face was taut, his expression bleak.

"Jesus, Katz, isn't there—"

"No," Katz interrupted. "There isn't a damn thing we can do for them. Except walk away, and then make sure this hellhole is laid to rest for good."

They moved down one of the branch corridors, searching for a way back down to ground level. Halfway along the corridor they came to a stairway, but it led only to an upper level.

As Katz and Manning approached the flight of steps, the crash of heavy boots sounded. A group of Mohn's troops burst into view at the top of the stairs. One of them caught sight of the Phoenix pair and yelled a warning to his companions. Even as he was raising the alarm, this Nazi opened fire with his AK-47, raking the area around Katz and Manning with ComBloc 7.62s. Bullets peppered the concrete wall of the passage, filling the air with stinging chips.

Gary Manning tracked his SA80 around, tilting the muzzle up toward the stairs. He opened fire, raking the group of Nazis with 5.56 flesh-shredders. The Enfield's rate of fire produced a burning stream of slugs that blasted the life out of two of the fanatics instantly, tossing them back against the others in the group. Desperately trying to bring their weapons into play, the Nazis shoved their dying comrades aside. The fatally hit men tumbled down the steep flight of stairs, trailing streams of blood.

Manning's swift response had given Katz time to bring his Uzi into the action. The Phoenix veteran triggered short bursts that punctured flesh and cracked bones. The screams of the dying Nazis rang out above the crackle of heavy autofire.

As the last enemy fell, Katz and Manning moved on past the stairway. Katz paused to prime a grenade, which he tossed to the top of the stairs. It exploded with a hefty crack, blowing a cloud of smoke across the hallway.

Rounding a corner then, the Phoenix warrior saw a door set in the wall ahead. "Let's try it," Katz said.

The door opened on what turned out to be an iron fire escape.

"I was beginning to think I'd never see daylight again," Manning said.

They began to descend the fire escape. From inside the building they could still hear the crackle of gunfire. When they were halfway down, the sound of an engine reached their ears.

Moments later a jeep holding four armed Nazis appeared and sped along the side of the building. One of the Nazis was standing behind what looked like an FN MAG 7.62 mm GPMG mounted on a swivel bracket. He was scanning the heights of the building, and there was no way he could have missed seeing Katz and Manning on the fire escape. He shouted no warning, but simply swung the FN MAG in the direction of the Phoenix warriors and opened fire.

The super commandos flattened themselves against the iron steps as a hail of 7.62s howled overhead, crashing viciously against the wall of the building. Other slugs clanged against the ironwork of the fire escape. If the jeep had been motionless the swift-acting gunner might have hit his targets. Luckily for Katz and Manning the gunner's aim was thrown off by the bounce of the moving vehicle, and then additionally so when the driver jammed on his brakes. Still, it was a tense moment.

When the long burst of fire trailed off, Manning pushed himself upright, poking his SA80 through the iron railings. He aimed quickly but accurately, triggering off a series of short bursts in the direction of the stalled vehicle. His second burst caught the driver full in the head, blowing his skull apart. Splintered bone flew through the air, followed by bits of brain.

The machine gunner, having recovered his balance, resighted his MAG and opened up again. Bullets zipped through the air around Manning. One of them clipped the sleeve of his combat jacket. Then something struck his right thigh, near the hip. It felt like someone kicking him hard with a heavy boot. Manning held his position, firing again, and was rewarded by the sight of a second occupant of the jeep tumbling out of the vehicle with a large red blotch appearing on his chest.

Katz, meanwhile, had pulled a couple of grenades from his satchel, yanked the pins and released the levers. Leaning over the edge of the fire escape, the Israeli commando tossed the round fragmentation grenades onto the jeep. The twin explosions were no more than a second apart. The jeep vanished in a mushroom of flame and smoke, then disappeared altogether as the fuel tank ignited. Writhing flames rose in the air, and debris pattered to the ground.

Pulling back from the railing, Manning rose to his feet—or so he intended. But he promptly fell. He slithered down half a dozen steps before he caught hold of the railing and hauled himself to a stop. Only then did he feel the savage burning in his thigh. Glancing down, he saw that his pantleg was sodden with blood.

"Damn!" he swore.

"Gary?" Katz crouched at his side.

"Looks like I caught one," Manning said through gritted teeth. The pain was spreading rapidly now.

Katz took a swift look at the area around the wound. He grunted to himself.

"What does that mean?" Manning asked.

"It means the bullet went right through," Katz said. "There's an exit hole in your pants."

"Good," Manning said. "Now let's get the hell off these damn stairs. I'm feeling very exposed."

The Israeli opened his mouth to speak, then paused, eyes suddenly alert. He turned, his Uzi following him around.

Two black-clad Nazis carrying AK-47s stood at the top of the fire escape. They were young, blond and extremely fit. But they were not combat veterans. They had not been in countless firefights where split-second timing meant the difference between living and dying.

Katz had, and he had learned to develop the sixth sense that made all the difference in an armed confrontation. While the two Nazis were still assessing the situation on the stairs, Katz had seen, registered, assessed—and responded. His Uzi stitched the pair with 9 mm terminators, a hot round of deadly bullets that cored into those too-slow brains and put them on eternal standby. The blond Nazis were thrown back, half on and half off the fire escape, blood and brains staining their once neat black uniforms.

Turning back to Manning, Katz said, "Let's go." He put out his right arm to offer support.

As they started down the fire escape a distant throb of sound reached them. Manning stared skyward, searching. Then, excitedly, he cried, "Over there, Katz."

They both watched as the dark spot in the sky grew bigger. It was drifting in toward the base, losing height as it approached. When it was close enough for identification, both Katz and Manning gave a sigh of relief. It was Dragon Slayer.

Dragon Slayer was here. Somehow, Jack Grimaldi and his chopper had found them.

Katz was smiling. Now the fight could really start.

KURT MOHN TURNED on the young captain, his anger so strong it almost seemed a physical force. "Well?" he demanded. "What is happening?"

The captain, Brunner by name, attempted to maintain his military decorum—which was difficult, under the circumstances. Everything seemed to be falling apart around their ears. The escaped American commandos were running amok all over the complex, taking out anyone who dared challenge them; they seemed to be indestructible.

In reality, Brunner had realized, the pair were that good because they were one hundred percent professionals—men who had spent their lives in various forms of combat. They walked into confrontations and handled them with ease, faced overwhelming odds and defeated them. As well as having reduced the ranks of the New Order, the American specialists were making a mockery of Mohn's ideals. His long-term training might have given his troops all the theory about combat and superiority, but in the face of *real* fighting men, those theories had proved to be little more than words on paper. The Mohn strategy might have worked against unarmed civilians, against the weak. But against determined opposition it had not fared well.

"Have you gone deaf?" Mohn yelled at Brunner.

Brunner shook his head. "No, sir," he replied.

"Then report."

"We have suffered a number of casualties. The native prisoners have been released and have obtained weapons. A short while ago they broke into the storage facility and exposed some of the contained Armageddon virus. A half a dozen of them, locked in the facility, were exposed to the virus and are dead. The Americans have left the building, but are somewhere within the perimeter. And a minute ago I received word that an unidentified helicopter is approaching the base."

"So," Mohn said, "we seem to be under siege. What would you suggest, Brunner?"

"The only thing we can do, sir, is resist. Otherwise these Americans will kill us all. I have given orders for the helicopter squad to intercept and destroy the unknown aircraft."

"Very good, Brunner," Mohn said. "There may be hope for you yet."

Mohn finished loading the H&K SMG he was carrying. He jammed a couple of extra magazines in his pocket. "Let's get this over with, Brunner. I've had enough of this foolishness." He turned to leave the office, then paused. "How are the engineers progressing with the armory door?"

"No success yet," Brunner said.

"No matter." Mohn had not informed anyone of the explosive charges set by the Americans. All he had told the engineers was that the door had been tampered with and needed to be opened so that extra weapons could be reached. If the engineers got through the door in time, all well and good. If they didn't . . .

"Are you with me, Brunner?" he asked.

Brunner nodded. Inwardly he was calling himself a fool to stay with Mohn, but he also realized he had nowhere else to go; he might as well be with Mohn as with any of the others. He would really rather have been back in Germany. At least there, his Nazi activities had remained fairly stable, if a little dull at times. The difference was that back home he would have been unlikely to have ever found himself in the middle of a bloody firefight, with people dying all around him and a madman who believed he was Adolf Hitler reincarnated leading them all into either glory or death. The fancy words and the fancier uniform Mohn provided all of a sudden didn't seem so appealing.

20

"Looks like a welcoming committee forming up," McCarter said.

"I see 'em," Grimaldi called back. He had already taken note of the helicopters preparing for lift-off.

"It sure is busy down there," said Calvin James, peering through one of the ports.

It was impossible to miss the activity taking place around the Nazi stronghold. Armed men were milling about, a number of them seemingly unsure of what they were supposed to be doing. A column of black smoke was rising from one side of the large building; due to Dragon Slayer's angle of approach, it was impossible for any of them to see what was causing the smoke.

"Hey!" Encizo called. "I know what caused all the fuss."

"What?" McCarter asked. He joined Encizo and was directed by the Cuban's pointing finger.

McCarter finally located the cause. It was Katz and Manning. He saw them moving across the compound, firing as they came. Katz appeared to be supporting Manning, who was limping heavily. Even as

McCarter spotted the pair, Manning went down. Katz instantly crouched over him, firing in the direction of an advancing trio of Nazi combat troops.

"To the right," McCarter yelled to Grimaldi.

"Got them," the pilot replied. He swung Dragon Slayer in a tight arc, bringing it on a heading that took it straight at the Nazi fanatics. Grimaldi's finger stroked the firing button and Dragon Slayer's multi-barrel cannon opened up, blasting a rain of 7.62 mm death at the Nazis. The intensity of the cannon fire ripped the three thugs apart, spreading their flesh and innards across the compound in a burst of crimson.

McCarter leaned over the back of Grimaldi's seat, his face tight with emotion. "Get us down there, Jack. They need us bloody quick."

Grimaldi nodded, his hands and feet working the combat chopper's controls as he took them down in a shallow dive, swinging Dragon Slayer around to face the oncoming New Order enemies. The helicopter hovered in a swirling cloud of dust.

First James leaped out, then Encizo. McCarter made a final check to see that Cavantes was securely cuffed to a body strut, then he, too, jumped out of the open hatch. The second the Phoenix warriors had exited the chopper Grimaldi resealed the hatch and swept Dragon Slayer back in the air, his mind already concentrating on the task that lay ahead of him.

One of the Hinds was already airborne. Two of the smaller Kiowa machines had just lifted off.

Grimaldi armed the rocket pods with HE missiles and drove Dragon Slayer in low and fast. He sighted in on the remaining helicopters. They were warming up, rotors beating the air. That was as far as they got. Grimaldi's missiles struck home, turning the chopper pad into a fiery maelstrom of flying metal and Plexiglas. Fuel and ammunition exploded, sending boiling flame skyward, taking with it the cremated remains of the Nazi pilots and gunners.

Satisfied that he had decimated the nonairborne helicopters, Grimaldi turned his attention to the three machines that had left the ground.

THE EXPLODING HELICOPTERS on the pad sent shock waves rippling out across the compound. The three Phoenix warriors felt the ground tremble as they sprinted toward Katz and Manning. James was in the lead, with Encizo only feet behind. McCarter was a few yards back, acting as rear guard to cover the others. The cockney's MAC-10 had already pushed back a couple of overeager fanatics.

As James and Encizo reached their Phoenix buddies they heard McCarter yell. Encizo glanced over his shoulder and saw that McCarter was pointing to his right. "Get them in there," the Brit called.

Encizo followed McCarter's finger. No more than twenty feet away was a deserted machine-gun emplacement—a circle of solid sandbags with the barrel of an FN MAG 7.62 machine gun poking over the lip.

"Calvin, grab Gary's other arm," Encizo snapped.

Together they manhandled the Canadian in the direction of the emplacement. Bullets zipped through the air. Others whacked the earth around their feet. Katz, carrying Manning's SA80, ran with them. The Phoenix team tumbled gratefully behind the protective cover of the sandbags, hearing the thud of bullets as they hit the sturdy wall.

Seconds later McCarter bounded over the top of the emplacement, a grin on his face. "This is nice," he said. "All back together again."

Encizo asked, "Katz, did you find out what was the secret project going on here?"

The Phoenix commander nodded. "Mohn has a bacteriological weapon he plans to use. A killer virus that will create havoc. He also has a mad scheme to start a worldwide Nazi revolution."

"The guy sounds a real nut case," McCarter muttered.

"We have to stop him and destroy that virus," Katz said. "But first we have to deal with this mess out here."

"I managed to set some plastic explosive before we got out," Manning told the newly arrived members of the team. "Should be ready to blow in a few minutes."

Calvin James had already cut open the blood-soaked pants around Manning's wound and made a quick examination of the entry and exit holes, nodding to himself. He found the necessary medication from his kit and began to clean the wound before applying pressure pads and a bandage.

"I'm going to be occupied for a while," the black warrior said, "so you go ahead without me."

"David, take that machine gun," Katz ordered.

McCarter nodded. He checked the weapon for ammunition before he snugged the MAG's butt to his shoulder. The Briton fired short, controlled bursts in the direction of the advancing New Order troops, scattering them. The main body of Nazis broke and ran for cover. Some of them caught 7.62 mm bonecrushers and were tumbled to the hard earth, where they kicked away their final moments in bloody agony.

While McCarter cleared one area with the MAG, Katz and Encizo fought off attacks coming from other directions. In the area of the compound Katz was covering, four Nazi thugs confronted him. They had broken from cover behind a parked jeep and were dashing in the direction of the emplacement, SMGs throwing a spray of slugs in the Israeli's direction. Sighting his Uzi, Katz fired off a long burst. The 9 mm slugs burned through the stomach of one fanatic and dropped him in the dirt. He rolled around in agony, clutching his ruptured torso, blood flowing through his fingers. Each time he moved, fresh waves of agony exploded within his body. He called out for his comrades, but they had run on, leaving him to die alone in the Amazon dust.

The moment he fired at the first Nazi, the Phoenix commander had shifted his aim, picking up on the other three in the group. One of them stopped running and plucked a grenade from his combat harness. He jerked out the pin and allowed the lever to spring free, but before he could draw back his arm to throw the grenade, Katz shot him, ripping a burst from his Uzi across the enemy's thighs. The chopping 9 mm slugs cleaved flesh and shattered the guy's leg bones, driving bone shards out through the pulpy exit wounds. With a startled cry the Nazi terrorist went down, unable to support himself on his mashed limbs. He hit the ground hard, his SMG spilling from his left hand. Although he wasn't aware of it, the primed grenade was still clutched in his right hand. It exploded with a powerful crash, and the Nazi's upper torso virtually vanished, blown out of existence by the force of the detonating grenade. His lacerated body jerked around in the bloody mess that remained.

The force of the blast knocked one of the two remaining Nazis off balance. He stumbled, hesitated as he tried to regain his balance. He was still trying when he felt a burning sensation in his chest. A fraction of a second later the burning became overwhelming pain that spread through his upper body, radiating so deep into his chest and increasing so much in intensity that his heart burst apart. It was only in the final moments of consciousness, as hot blood rushed from the hole in his chest, that the fanatic realized he had been shot. A rapid burst of fire from Katz's Uzi had drilled 9 mm slugs into his flesh. The Nazi stumbled again, this time falling facedown in the dirt, finding out what it was like to die.

As the third man went down, Katz turned his attention and his Uzi on the last surviving member of the quartet. This one had used his comrade's final moments as a means of diverting Katz's deadly weapon away from himself. He ducked and weaved as he ran, putting on a burst of speed that was impressive. It brought him to within ten feet of the emplacement. He was silently congratulating himself on reaching his objective, when he was abruptly confronted by a middle-aged man of mild appearance who showed himself above the top of the sandbags. For a second the Nazi, who considered himself a perfect Aryan specimen, refused to believe that this *old* man was one of the group that had invaded the secret base, causing so much damage and confusion. How could such an individual have been instrumental in causing the deaths of so many of the New Order troopers? he wondered.

The "old" man swung an Uzi SMG into view, the dark muzzle lining up on the Nazi with absolute precision. Katz pulled the trigger and sent the enemy's life from his body with a single sustained blast that tore heart and lungs to shreds, blowing them out through the exit holes that appeared between the shoulders in a spray of bloody gore. The Nazi superman was driven to the ground by the force of the blast, where he lay kicking and twitching in a most un-Aryan way.

Dropping back behind the sandbags for a few seconds, Katz slammed a fresh magazine of 9 mm ammo into the Uzi. He took a look at his watch and saw that the time was approaching for the explosion of the charges Manning had set in the basement armory.

"Everybody, keep your heads down. Gary's big blast should be happening just about—"

Katz's words were drowned by the thunderous roar of the charges going off and igniting the rest of the explosives stored in the basement of the building. Although much of the blast's force was contained in the basement area, with flame and smoke billowing out along the corridors and wiping out any life within a wide area, enough of the devastating explosion rose up from the basement to blow out a corner and part of one side wall of the building. As this occurred on the ground level, the resultant weakening of the main structure caused major cracks to split open the outer wall above the fracture. Windows cracked and burst from their frames. Floors caved in and stairways collapsed. Severed power cables danced about, causing short circuits and in some places fires.

In addition, debris from the building, comprising concrete, metal and glass, was blown in all directions. What was blown straight up in the air rained down again in a deadly shower across the compound. Other pieces of the structure were blown across the compound with the force of cannonballs. For a few hectic, terrifying seconds, the area around the building became an extremely dangerous place. More than one of Kurt Mohn's New Order troopers became instant mincemeat. Arms and legs were ripped from bodies. One blond Aryan was decapitated by a glittering plate of shiny steel as it scythed across the compound. There was still a look of utter astonishment on the dead Nazi's face as his severed head bounced across the compound, trailing bloody strings in its wake.

Part of the wall of sandbags fell in on Phoenix Force as the hot blast of the explosion blew over their place of shelter. Thanks to Katz's timely warning, the Stony Man warriors escaped unhurt, apart from a few minor cuts and bruises.

"Calvin, can you contact Jack on that thing?" Katz asked, indicating the radio communicator still clipped to James's belt.

James nodded. "Yeah," he said. "I set it to Jack's frequency before we left Dragon Slayer."

"Good," the Israeli said. "Get through to him now. I want him to lay everything he's got into that building. He's to destroy it entirely. Tell him to use his white-phosphorous rockets to burn out that eastern corner section. That's where the virus is stored."

McCarter discarded the FN MAG and picked up his MAC-10. The Brit's face, streaked with dirt, was set hard as he said, "Let's go and finish off this bunch of miserable bastards. I've had enough of this bleeding jungle."

"I'm with you," Encizo said, hefting his H&K MP-5. The Phoenix pair vaulted over the broken line of sandbags and separated as they moved across the smoke-streaked compound.

Encizo spotted a trio of New Order supermen. The Nazi fanatics were armed to the teeth, faces wild with rage as they sought the ones responsible for destroying their fantasy. One of them caught sight of the Cuban as he emerged from the drifting smoke. The Nazi called to his two comrades, and pointed out Encizo.

Without waiting for his partners to back him, one of the New Order soldiers darted forward, swinging up his AK-47, already congratulating himself on the slaying of one of the invaders. He was still giving himself a mental pat on the back when Encizo's MP-5 burst into life. A flesh-shredding stream of 9 mm slugs streaked across the space between Encizo and his target. The Nazi was driven back across the compound, his body alive with pain as Encizo's bullets tore open his flesh and started his life's blood draining into the Amazonian dirt. The fanatic crashed to the ground and died in his own gore.

As soon as he had triggered the burst at the first Nazi, Encizo turned toward the other pair, who had been a little slower to react. They were still bringing the muzzles of their weapons around when Encizo locked on target and canceled their membership in the Nazi party for eternity. They danced their death jig together, blood spurting from their ruptured torsos in glistening streams. Then they lay still in an inelegant, heavy and inert sprawl, like clumps of lifeless clay.

David McCarter, meanwhile, found himself face-to-face with a single Nazi fanatic, who emerged from behind an overturned jeep, cradling an FN MAG in his powerful arms. He had a deep gash in his head, from which blood was pouring down his face. Despite this he walked with a determined step toward the ex-SAS man, his fingers busily threading an ammunition belt into the MAG.

"Give it up, mate," the Brit called. "You hear me?"

"Go to hell, you blithering idiot!" the blond German yelled in his accented English. "I will kill you before I surrender." As he spoke, the Nazi completed his loading. He cocked the heavy weapon, bringing it around to bear on McCarter.

The cockney sighed with resignation, triggering the MAC-10, which he had already aimed at the German. The Ingram stuttered loudly, driving 9 mm slugs deep into the fanatic's bulk. The German terrorist screamed loudly as the round chewed his internal organs to mush and his blood flowed freely from the wounds, soaking his clothing.

McCarter moved on, seeking fresh targets, as the Nazi slumped to the ground, already well on his way into the endless sleep of death.

BY THE TIME the explosion in the armory took place, partially wrecking Kurt Mohn's building, Jack Grimaldi had already eliminated one of the Kiowa helicopters. The small craft, though fast and capable of energetic moves, had been unable to shake off Dragon Slayer.

The combat chopper from Stony Man was not only a larger aircraft, but its computer-designed fuselage concealed the power unit of a helicopter devised as the ultimate fighting machine. Dragon Slayer was ahead of its time. The sleek, black body had been scientifically streamlined to offer the least possible wind resistance, while still retaining enough body surface to remain stable under any conditions created during flight. Dragon Slayer's controls were supersensitive, giving Grimaldi the instant, total response and control over his machine's performance that was vital in a combat situation. A pilot needed his aircraft to respond almost as fast as he thought. Delay of even a few seconds could mean the difference between life and death.

Grimaldi was finding out now just how good Dragon Slayer was as he threw the powerful combat chopper around the wide Amazonian sky. The aircraft had become an extension of himself. It moved as he moved, turned and twisted and rolled even as he thought the maneuvers. The instant responses he was able to elicit from the helicopter provided Grimaldi with near-total superiority in the air.

He took out the first Kiowa with a sustained burst from his rotary cannon, the 7.62s shredding the enemy chopper's Plexiglas canopy and almost cutting the pilot in half. The out-of-control Kiowa spun off at an angle, twisting end over end before it vanished in a rolling fireball as it hit the jungle floor.

Aware of the presence of the other two New Order helicopters, Grimaldi took Dragon Slayer in a dizzying climb at full throttle. When he leveled off he could see the Kiowa and the Hind far below. A burst of flame from beneath the Hind signaled the release of one of its heat-seeking missiles.

Grimaldi's fingers touched his control panel, exposing and arming one of the Sunburst missiles; this was an antimissile missile, designed to explode and disperse flaring charges in a wide pattern in the path of an incoming projectile. The Sunburst's charges were heat producing, designed to attract the heat-seeking enemy missile by offering substitute heat sources. Grimaldi locked Dragon Slayer's inbuilt computer onto the Hind's missile, and it quickly calculated a flight path for the Sunburst, then triggered the missile. Grimaldi watched it curve in toward the incoming heat-seeker. There was a bright flare of spiraling heat spots as the Sunburst hatched its eggs. The Hind's missile altered course as its sensors told it the heat source was present. Locking in on one of the bright decoy stars, the Hind's missile exploded harmlessly.

Still high above his adversaries, Grimaldi launched one of his own HE missiles and watched it streak down and turn the remaining Kiowa into a pulsing fireball. Then he worked the controls and took Dragon Slayer down in a power dive directly over the Hind. The

Hind's pilot, suddenly aware of the threat from above, initiated evasive action. The Russian chopper lumbered back and forth across the clear Amazonian sky, desperately trying to shake off the persistent Dragon Slayer. The New Order pilot, who was no beginner when it came to flying helicopters, realized he was being pursued by a better machine, which was piloted by a better man.

Concentrating on placing himself in a prime position for an attack, Grimaldi picked up a voice coming in over his headset. There was a lot of static, but the Stony Man flier recognized the voice of Calvin James.

"Dragon Slayer, acknowledge. Acknowledge," James repeated.

"I hear you, over," Grimaldi responded.

"We need your firepower, Dragon Slayer. Lay it all on the building. Phosphorous rockets into the east upper corner. It has to be burned clean. Germ virus needs eliminating. Over."

"I read you," Grimaldi answered. "I'll handle it. Over and out."

He cut the connection, then turned his attention back to the Hind, aware that this part of the game had to be terminated fast.

Jack Grimaldi pulled out all the stops, using the second-nature skills that made him one of the best combat pilots alive. He put Dragon Slayer behind the Hind and held it there while he made his firing assessment. Touching the button, he opened up with the rotary cannon, blasting a long burst of 7.62s into the

Hind's engine compartment. He kept up the fire until he saw the Soviet ship's body blow open. A thick stream of black smoke, mixed with hot oil, belched from the stricken engine. Seconds later there was a burst of flame that swelled and expanded. The Hind began to falter as the rotors stuttered, slowed. The heavy machine sank quickly, tilting to one side. It hit the ground nose first, crumpling like a deflating balloon. The explosion that followed was spectacular, fuel erupting in a shimmering ball, while exploding ammunition created a rippling fireworks effect.

Grimaldi gunned his black combat chopper around and headed toward the partly demolished building. He took in the devastation covering the compound, noticed the sprawled bodies of the dead. That would be Phoenix Force, carrying out their part of the mission with customary zeal and thoroughness. When he saw the results of a Phoenix Force attack, Grimaldi was damned glad he was on their side.

Dragon Slayer hovered before the building. Grimaldi fed data into the on-board computer and it locked on, its sensors scanning the building. He activated the remaining phosphorous missiles while he waited for the computer to feed the flight paths into the missile memories. The moment the computer gave him the green light, Grimaldi let the missiles go, watching their flight.

The missiles—five of them—drove deep into the building and exploded into brilliant white balls of intense heat as the exposed phosphorous did its deadly work.

Turning Dragon Slayer slightly, Grimaldi used his last HE missiles to bring down more of Kurt Mohn's jungle headquarters.

21

The young Nazi named Brunner was close to one of the outer walls of the complex when Grimaldi's final salvo of HE missiles struck. The exploding rockets blew great chunks of concrete from the building's structure. Brunner was slammed to the ground, his body aching from the concussion. Blood filled his mouth from where he had bitten his tongue, and he could feel a raw graze down the left side of his face. He lay where he was for a few moments, trying to bring his shattered senses back into some sort of order.

All around him he could hear the noises of battle—the hammer and rattle of gunfire, the thud of exploding grenades, the yells of anger and the screams of pain.

Some minutes back he had lost contact with Kurt Mohn. In the confusion of fire and smoke and sudden death they had drifted apart. Brunner had made no attempt to contact Mohn again. In a way he was glad to be away from the madman. He had come to realize now the reality of Mohn's lunacy. Before, working for the New Order had all seemed like a grand game, some fantastic charade in which they all got to parade around in fine uniforms, sporting the gleaming weapons they fired off so regularly at the basement shooting range.

Then suddenly—without warning—everything had changed. The game had turned cold and the world had taken on a grimness that had shocked Brunner. He had watched men die before his eyes—men he had trained with, had laughed and joked with. Men of high ideals, like himself, all puffed up with the myths and legends of Hitler's Reich. Mohn had driven it into them day and night—how they would march in glorious conquest and redeem all those Nazi heroes of years gone by. They had listened and they had cheered themselves hoarse. For weeks, for months, they had trained and studied, they had planned and they had schemed, all for the big day. For the day of Armageddon, when the New Order would shock the world into wide-eyed astonishment as it stepped in and took over.

Now a bitter laugh bubbled from Brunner's lips. Take over the world? The New Order couldn't even handle a small team of American commandos. This five-man group had exploded among the New Order's troops and instructors, and had almost eliminated them. They had shown the Nazi force that all the will in the world, all the weaponry, meant nothing when it was faced by true and dedicated professional warriors.

Captain Brunner gathered himself and pushed shakily to his feet. There was no question now that they had been beaten by a superior force. And if they didn't keep fighting they would *all* be wiped out. Brunner would have preferred to drop his weapon and run. But where was there to run? All that lay beyond the perimeter of the compound was jungle, mile upon trackless mile of it. And none of them had any real idea where they were. They had always been flown in and out blind, at night, with no radio contact for fear of being monitored. They were lost in the middle of the Amazon rain forest with nowhere to go. So they might as well keep on fighting, in case some miracle happened and they won.

Crouching, Brunner scanned the area. He spotted a tight group of black-clad troopers beside an over-turned jeep and scuttled across to them. There were five in the group. They glanced at him with questions in their eyes he couldn't answer.

"So, Captain Brunner," a hulking blond called Krieg sneered, "any bright ideas rolling around in that pretty head of yours?"

"Only one, Krieg," Brunner answered. "That we need to stay alive. And the only chance we have of doing that is to fight our way out of this bloody mess."

Krieg chuckled. "Brilliant," he said. "I can see how you got to be a captain!"

"So what's *your* answer?" Brunner asked, refusing to be intimidated by Krieg. The man was bully, a tormentor of his fellows—that was when he wasn't trying to get them into his bed. It was a well-known fact around the barracks that Krieg was an ardent pursuer of his Aryan brethren.

The big German clicked a fresh magazine into his AK-47 and worked the bolt with a vicious snap. "I'll show you what I'm going to do," he said. "No damned American gangsters are scaring me off."

Krieg broke away from the cover of the jeep, moving across the compound in the direction of the only remaining vehicle that was still on its wheels. Although impressed by his big comrade's zeal, Brunner had some difficulty mustering a similar feeling at this late stage of the game. Nonetheless, he turned to his charges. "Cover him," he ordered, and they—still retaining enough of the Nazi mentality—obeyed without question. Then they fanned out from the derelict jeep, weapons up and ready, and took off after Krieg. Brunner checked his own weapon and reluctantly followed them. He just hoped they had enough luck left between them to pull off Krieg's plan. He didn't hold out much hope.

CALVIN JAMES HAD SETTLED Manning back against the stacked sandbags. The Canadian was conscious, but the painkiller James had injected had left him drowsy. Despite his condition, however, he insisted on hanging on to his SA80.

Katz, who had remained inside the emplacement with James to keep watch while the black medic tended to Manning, suddenly snapped, "Calvin, quick!"

Snatching up his M-16, James joined the Israeli and followed Katz's pointing finger.

A tall, powerful-looking New Order trooper was making a dash for a jeep stranded in the middle of the compound. Emerging from behind an overturned vehicle were a number of other Nazis. They fanned out as they cleared the vehicle, a couple of them raising their weapons at the exposed backs of McCarter and Encizo, who were facing the other way.

"No, you don't, you bastards," James muttered. He snapped the M-16 to his shoulder and sighted in on one of the would-be shooters-in-the-back. The weapon cracked, spitting 5.56 mm objectors to the Nazis' plan. The closest of the opponents caught a trio of slugs in his chest. The 5.56s ripped into his flesh, crashing through bone, seeking refuge in the heart. He stumbled back, the massive shock of the wound rendering him speechless. Within seconds he was dead, his heart pulverized by the impact of the M-16.

Even as James's finger was easing back the trigger of his M-16, Katz, beside him, had already locked on to his target. The Uzi in his hand ripped off a sharp burst that sent 9mm slugs coring into the head of the second Nazi. It was fine shooting over the distance; Katz was no slouch when it came to taking out vermin. Spun around by the force of the bullets from Katz's weapon, the terrorist lost his balance and flopped to the ground, his shattered skull emptying his brains over the earth.

Alerted by the gunfire, McCarter and Encizo about faced, assessing the situation in an instant. They saw what their Phoenix buddies had done to cut down the odds, and pitched in themselves to reduce them further.

McCarter dropped to one knee, reducing the amount of target the Nazis had to shoot at. He whipped up his MAC-10 and blew another of the running enemies off his feet. The surprised fanatic jerked back on the trigger of his Kalashnikov as McCarter's bullets struck home, his weapon discharging its load into the dirt. Moments later he, too, was in the dirt, facedown, kicking and squirming in agony, with a gut full of McCarter's slugs.

In the meantime Encizo had turned his H&K loose on the other two. One of them, he noticed almost casually, was wearing the insignia of a *Hauptsturm-fuhrer*—a captain. Not that rank made any difference in this instance. The guy was armed and offering resistance. A terrorist was a terrorist, no matter how he dressed up the part. As he completed his turn, Encizo saw that the lead Nazi was already in the act of firing his AK-47. The Cuban arched his supple body around, throwing himself to the earth. He hit on one shoulder, absorbing the impact as he allowed himself to roll over. Dimly he heard the AK-47's bullets thunk into the ground just beyond him. Then Encizo brought himself into position, his H&K thrust forward and up. He pulled back on the MP-5's trigger, throwing a 9 mm spray in the direction of the two Nazis. His aim was on target and the pair of New Order puppets performed to a different set of instructions as Encizo's long burst riddled them with burning flesh-shredders.

The black uniforms were suddenly patterned with red. The fanatics tumbled to the ground in sprays of blood, twitching and protesting at the way life was being wrenched from them. But they were too late, there was no backing out of the game at that late stage.

THE DEMISE OF HIS COMRADES had given Krieg the time to reach the abandoned jeep. With an exultant cry the big Nazi leaped up on the back of the vehicle, reaching for the MAG mounted there. He grabbed the handgrips and swung the machine gun in the direction of the emplacement. Jerking back on the trigger, Krieg sent a stream of slugs marching across the compound. When he saw he was falling short, he raised the barrel. Again he fired and this time saw his shots ripping into the sandbags. Grinning widely, he settled the butt of the MAG against his shoulder and fired again. The 7.62 mm slugs began to shred the bags of sand. "Show your goddamn heads!" Krieg yelled. "Yankee bastards! Show your heads and I'll blow them off!"

McCarter was pulling a fresh magazine from his belt and ramming it into the MAC-10, and a few yards away Encizo was climbing to his feet, when the hammer of the FN MAG blasting out its 7.62 melody caught the attention of the Phoenix pros.

"Where did that sneaky bugger pop up from?" McCarter asked as he spotted Krieg. The Brit didn't wait for an answer. He ran forward, the MAC-10 adding its sound to the din of the MAG. His first blast smacked into the jeep's front wheel and hood.

Alerted, Krieg threw a glance at McCarter. He laughed as he saw the ex-SAS man dashing in his direction. Hauling the MAG around on its swivel, Krieg lined it up on McCarter.

But McCarter fired first, and this time he took better aim. His stream of slugs caught Krieg in the left arm and shoulder, ripping open flesh and muscle, shattering bone. The impact pulled the massive German away from the machine gun. He almost lost his balance but kept a grip on the MAG. Despite the pulped and gory mess that had been his arm and shoulder, he made a further attempt to fire back.

He might have managed to do so if Encizo hadn't opened fire, too. His H&K sent a volley of shots into the jeep's bodywork. There was a dull thump as the fuel tank blew. A sheet of flame engulfed the jeep.

Seconds later something detached itself from the fireball. It was Krieg, his body a mass of boiling flame. He stumbled as his feet hit the ground, his arms flailing as he tried vainly to extinguish the searing fire that was bubbling and frying his flesh. His shrill screams rang out across the littered compound. They went on and on as the burning man thrashed aimlessly about, and then ceased abruptly when David McCarter emptied his MAC-10 into the suffering Nazi's body. Krieg crashed to the ground and lay still, the flames continuing to devour his corpse.

Almost as if someone had thrown a switch, all activity ceased. A heavy silence descended, broken only by the soft moans of the wounded and dying.

Phoenix Force regrouped, aware that resistance had ended. The lull brought a tension all its own. Each man stared around, not trusting the quiet, expecting violent action to break out again at any second.

It didn't.

There was no one left to fight.

A few minutes later Dragon Slayer swung into sight and came in for a landing. As soon as it touched down Gary Manning was carried over to the combat chopper and made comfortable inside.

One by one the surviving Indians came out of hiding and stood staring at Dragon Slayer. There were no more than a half dozen of them left. They made no attempt to come any closer to the helicopter or Phoenix Force, and soon after that they drifted away from the compound and vanished in the jungle.

Inside the helicopter Katz asked Grimaldi to patch him through to Stony Man, via the satellite link they were able to use. It took some time, but finally Katz was able to speak to Hal Brognola over a reasonably clear line.

"How goes it?" the Fed asked gruffly.

"As far as we can tell, the mission is complete," Katz said. "We can't be positive Mohn is eliminated, because he was not among the dead we've found, but there was a sizeable explosion and fire in his complex, and it's likely he was incinerated there."

"Is everybody okay?" was Brognola's next question.

"Yes," Katz answered. "One minor injury but I think the patient will pull through."

In the main part of the helicopter Gary Manning gave a grunt of annoyance. "Minor, he calls it."

"Yeah, but he did say you'll pull through," McCarter pointed out. "You're lucky. He never even mentioned my scratch."

"Can I inform the Man the situation is stable?" Brognola asked Katz.

"As far as we can tell," Katz said. "We have a prisoner for the head man over here. He can point the finger at some people who have been indiscreet. It should help clean house."

"Great," Brognola said. "Wrap it up, guys. Come on home."

"And that," McCarter said, "is the best thing I've heard for days!"

For once no one disagreed with his opinion.

EPILOGUE

He had slipped away during the last few minutes of the conflict, aware that this time he had to concede defeat. The thought angered him, left a bitter taste in his mouth. He compromised and called his flight a strategic withdrawal. He would return one day, and when he did he would have his revenge on the five men who had destroyed his dream.

What enraged him most was the destruction of all that his late father had strived for. All that he—Kurt Mohn—had been living for: the rebirth of the Reich.

In a new form. With new ideas. But with the same end.

For now that dream would have to be denied him. But there would be another time, another day. Too much had been pinned on his grand scheme. It could not—would not—be allowed to die.

He would establish a new base somewhere else. He had the connections. He had the money—millions locked away from the drug sales, from the donations, from Mohn industries. He would lose the companies now—he accepted that. They had only been a means to an end, anyway; in themselves, they had meant nothing to him. Now that phase of his life was over, and a new start was called for.

He lay concealed in the dense undergrowth, watching, waiting. His body burned with pain from the injuries he had sustained during the final destruction of his complex, when the rockets from that damned helicopter had torn it down. The pain only intensified his anger. Fueled his desire for vengeance and for the reestablishment of his New Order. New Order or whatever, he thought. One thing for sure—in a world where so many wanted to be led, he knew he was born to rule!

Phoenix Force—bonded in secrecy to avenge the acts of terrorists everywhere.

Super Phoenix Force #2

American ''killer'' mercenaries are involved in a KGB plot to overthrow the government of a South Pacific island. The American President, anxious to preserve his country's image and not disturb the precarious position of the island nation's government, sends in the experts—Phoenix Force—to prevent a coup.

A secret consortium conspires to terrorize the world

DON PENDLETON's
MACK BOLAN

Tightrope

One by one, the top officials of international intelligence agencies are murdered, spearheading a new wave of terrorist atrocities throughout Western Europe. Mack Bolan's mission is compromised from the start. The line between good and evil is a tightrope no man should walk. Unless that man is the Executioner.

TAKE 'EM NOW

FOLDING SUNGLASSES FROM GOLD EAGLE

Mean up your act with these tough, street-smart shades. Practical, too, because they fold 3 times into a handy, zip-up polyurethane pouch that fits neatly into your pocket. Rugged metal frame. Scratch-resistant acrylic lenses. Best of all, they can be yours for only $6.99.

MAIL YOUR ORDER TODAY.

Send your name, address, and zip code, along with a check or money order for just $6.99 + .75¢ for postage and handling (for a total of $7.74) payable to Gold Eagle Reader Service. (New York and Iowa residents please add applicable sales tax.)

Remove from pouch...

unfold once...

GOLD EAGLE
Gold Eagle Reader Service
901 Fuhrmann Blvd.
P.O. Box 1396
Buffalo, N.Y. 14240-1396

unfold twice...

and they're ready to wear.

GES-1A

Offer not available in Canada.